Ballad of a Stonepicker

a novel by George Ryga

copyright © 1976 George Ryga

Talonbooks
201 1019 East Cordova
Vancouver
British Columbia V6A 1M8
Canada

This book was typeset by Linda Gilbert of B.C. Monthly Typesetting Service, designed by David Robinson and printed by Web Offset for Talonbooks.

Editor: Karl Siegler

First printing: December 1976

This book was first published in England by Michael Joseph Ltd. in 1966. It is a revised edition.

Canadian Cataloguing in Publication Data

Ryga, George, 1932-
    Ballad of a stonepicker

    ISBN 0-88922-110-3 pa.

    I. Title.
PS8585   C813'.5'4   C77-002033-X
PR9199.3

Now what is it you've come to see me about? I have your letter — it came on Tuesday. I was going to reply, but there is so much to do here . . . Yes, you wrote about Jim, having known him as a friend.

I agree it was something for him to become a Rhodes scholar. Not many of those around, and damned few ever make it from a place such as this. Oh, it's not a bad place as places go. Not a helluva lot for the mind, but when it rains like it's been doing the past two days there's bound to be things growing. Maybe I exaggerate saying that, but I've got to believe in something.

Yes, I know in a couple of months it'll be that time of year again when he died. Always someone or something to remind me . . . I wonder if it will ever end? From what you said in your letter, I understand you will be writing a story or article for some magazine about my brother — yes? And you want me to tell you everything! In two hours . . . maybe three if I talk slow!

Don't look at me that way. I'm not angry. I'm just tired. You see, there's nothing more to tell. The way I see it, the two things which made my brother Jim important to guys like yourself is that he came from such a place as this, and that he died when he did. That's all. I can't tell you more than you already know about him. If you were his friend, you know more than I do. If you want to know what sort of people Jim came up from — what it cost the family to educate him and what his death did to them and to me — that's another story. You see . . . I want to leave this place but I can't. His death did that to me. I'm all that's left, me and the debts taken out to educate him. I'm paying my brother's debts, buddy. I'll be paying them for the rest of my life. For two years now, I've been losing ground with bad health and poor crops. All I've been able to pay off is the interest on the money owing.

But it'll be better. This rain will help. And I'm feeling pretty good healthwise these days. Come on in — no sense standing out here in the rain.

On a clear day I would take you for a walk up Windy Hill. From there you could see all there is to see. You could take four pictures from there and say, "that's all there's to it." Or you might want to stay a while and have a quick look at the fields I'm working. Which isn't much, but it's better than nothing.

I shouldn't talk like that. It's a habit I have . . . I get nervous talking to someone for the first time. You're not dressed for walking up any hill, and the road's too muddy for driving up there. Come inside — I'll make us tea. House is in a mess. Nothing's been done to clean it from front door to back since my mother went away. That bedroom used to be hers and it hasn't been swept since she left. Look at the tub of dishes, will you! I can't find time to keep up with them, even when it rains. I wash them on Saturdays. All week they pile up. I've got seven each of plates, spoons, forks and knives — for the seven days of the week. This time of year when the weather's warm and I'm working outside, breakfast is the only meal I eat in the house. I boil up a few eggs and take some bread and coffee to where I work. By the time I get back, it's turning dark, and most days I feel so tired from the sun and wind I don't feel like cooking. So I go to bed.

Here, have a chair.

It's not often I have visitors now. Used to be different once. This kitchen has always been a kitchen and sitting room. A lot of neighbours came visiting when my old man was around. Surrounded by people he knew, he was a good, entertaining talker. He was shy with strangers, but with

people he liked — I've seen him in that chair over there carrying on three conversations with three different men at the
same time, mixing up their memories of old songs, tired
feet and bargains in farm machinery. When he'd got them
all properly screwed up, he'd say over his shoulder —

"Hey, mama! You making tea? . . . Pour my cup first if
you are. That fancy new tea you bought makes my heart
jump if it's brewed longer than thirty seconds!"

The men laughed and he laughed, and she poured his
cup first like he asked her to. There was nothing wrong
with her tea. It was his house and he wanted her to serve
him first . . .

While the water's warming I'll show you pictures of the
old man. There's a couple taken when he still had all his
teeth in. After that he had them all pulled one winter when
he got this gum infection. He'd planned to buy dental plates
but there was always something needed buying first. So
when he laughed he used to cover his mouth with a handkerchief, and my mother put his meat through the grinder
after she'd cooked it.

You get paid for coming here? . . . I thought so.

No matter how hard a man works, there's never enough
money to pay what's owing. Even when Jim was still here,
we were always broke. Always something that hadn't been
paid for and the store we bought groceries from on time
was always hollering — pay up or we'll see you in court!
Those memories never leave you — the shame of unworthi-
ness, the feeling of not being able to provide food and
clothing for yourself no matter how much work you do.
It stays with you like a numb headache. I'm cutting wood
and I still get scared of snagging my pants because it's the
only pair I can afford between now and the next winter.
Last few years I've been wearing canvas running shoes such
as these, which I buy for a dollar and a half at the sports
store in town. I walk through a pair a month, but it comes
out cheaper than leather boots in the long run.

I can see in your eyes you're not really interested in my problems. Why should you be? . . . Look out the window. It's nice-looking country when the rain stops. Air is fresh and when it's hot and dry there's always a smoke-haze in the atmosphere. A truck going down the gravel road into town raises dust that don't settle for half an hour. It's because of this clay — the same clay you can't walk through when it gets wet won't stay down when it dries into dust.

I met a guy once who told me parts of Australia were like that. I don't know about that. I've never been to Australia. Never been more than twenty miles from this house. Don't intend to go, either. There's enough to do and see right here. Besides, I'm too old.

Sure, I'm twenty-eight. But over here you can be old at twenty. My brother didn't age that way, but then Jim didn't have to live here all that long. My mother was grey before she reached twenty-five. And the old man lost his teeth at my age. When he died he was forty-three years old. Yet there are days when this country makes you forget all that. I've seen this blue haze on a hot day — the sun going low in the west and a blackbird flying against the evening light like it was shot from an arrow. You see a thing like that and you say to yourself there's some things in this world are all right.

I still remember the trees and scrub which grew here once. It was all taken out by hand — every branch and root. Underneath was grey earth. And in the earth the stones. They call us "dirt farmers" here in the backlands. Not because we're dirtier than farmers anywhere else, but because we've got to keep our hands closer to the soil to keep going. Winters are cold here. At thirty-five below you can hear the poplars explode with frost. Spring turns up fresh blisters of stone which weren't there the summer before. Then comes heat, and the dust and the mud when it rains. It's not the best way to live, but it's a way . . .

The last member of parliament from these parts was a

lawyer who called us red bastards because he didn't get our votes. Nobody gets our votes unless he comes out here and talks to us straight off the chest in language we understand. A man don't have to do more than open his mouth and we know if he's real or not. We gave our votes one time to a man who couldn't even make a speech. He stood up in Anderson's Hall, shrugged and pawed around with his feet, then said —

"If I get in there, I'll tell 'em we got to have better roads an' a bit of education for the kids!"

We gave him all our votes. It's the only votes he got, but he got them. The guy who won was this lawyer who never even came to see us.

But you came all this way to ask about my brother . . . He's dead. He's not here anymore. All that's left of his blood and memories is me. And this farm, and the people he grew up among. Maybe that's all that's left to tell. And once it's told no more need be said ever again. For you who's come all this way from the city it may not even be very interesting. It's too wet for me to do any work outside, and the dishes can wait another day. So if you want to listen, I'll tell you everything I know. But I can't tell about Jim without telling about everybody. It's the way life is lived here. There was never a lock on that door. We grew up on everybody's knee. Jim and I never really saw eye to eye on much. We couldn't. But life made us what we are, and I'm the only one left to tell about it . . .

My brother was a year and a half younger than me, but he was always brighter. In school, Jim put everything he had into his books. I got my head turned around easy by a cowboy song or a dirty joke, but not Jim. By grade three, he'd got ahead of me in school. And when I got to the sixth grade he was through the eighth and was starting high school in town. My folks never *said* it was no point in me pushing on, but I knew what they thought. When I didn't go back to school for grade seven they never once spoke to me about it. I know it was my fault for quitting — but I had other reasons.

Today, as then, I wonder what was the point of me going on, if all school was doing for me was giving me a place to grow bigger than other kids in the same grade — bigger even than the teacher. I was always hungry, so I ate a lot and grew bigger and bigger. I used to slouch so I'd look smaller. I'd try only half as hard in the games to keep from winning all the time. But there were times some kid would get hurt, and I'd be blamed because I was *bigger* and was somehow responsible. I hated what was happening in my body. It was like a prison growing up around me, forcing the man inside to feel and think like the body of the man outside was expected to perform. My brother was small and you're a small man yourself — perhaps it's not important to anyone else. It's important to me because a lot of the good things and bad things in my life keep going back to that . . .

Water's boiling. Would you prefer coffee to tea? I would. We'll eat together in a few hours, but coffee first — eh?

I make good coffee which you can smell as far as the road. A fistful of coffee in the pot, then scald it with boiling water and let it steep for ten minutes. Best coffee you'll ever drink! My old man made it that way — that's how I learned. He made his own coffee on nights when mama went to bed and he still stayed up talking or arguing with a neighbour. I'd wake after my first sleep — hungry, with the smell of his coffee all over the house. I wasn't allowed to get up. So I'd lay back and keep swallowing and listening. Sometimes I'd hear him humming some old song. Other times he was laughing and talking low. And one night I heard him argue with John, the wife-beater, who must've come late 'cause he hadn't been visiting when I went to bed.

"Turn yourself in before she does. You're crazy coming here!" my old man said in a loud voice. John was whining like a kid. That was how he was — first he'd whine and then he'd cry, but when his wife had to be beaten, he'd do a proper job of it.

"I can't. They'd give me three months in jail this time an' I got to get the crop in!"

I heard him cough. I sat up in bed when he kept on coughing for I knew he was crying.

"One day they'll put you in and you'll stay in — you know that!" My father's voice was lower, less angry now. "Here. Drink this."

I heard the wife-beater clink his spoon against a cup.

"You're right . . . you're right . . ."

"What'd you do this time? Put her in hospital?"

"Hell, no. It'd take three men to beat her into a hospital. I tied her up to the fence an' whipped her with a rope. Not badly — just across the back an' bottom end!"

"A rope?" My father's voice rose again. "What do you think the woman is — a goddamned cow?"

"No, she's not a cow! I just beat her with a rope . . . a wet rope, to teach her a lesson. What else can I do? God doesn't see what goes on, neither do you! Cold beans for supper . . . burned eggs for breakfast. Complain an' she's off at the mouth like a runaway hay-mower!"

A lot of men beat their wives — at least two besides him were pretty mean about it. But John always went over-board with the business. It could never be kept at home with him. After he'd almost half-kill her, he'd go out to whine and cry to somebody about it. In the meantime she'd always find the strength to crawl into town and turn him in to the police.

So John put in and took off two crops a year. One on his own farm and the other at the provincial jail farm where he served time twice a year for at least ten years.

Yet it all ended this last time he went in. For when he came out she'd run off with another man, a hired hand who was remembered for eating lots of salt with his food. I can't even remember his name now, only that he ate lots

13

of salt. She never came back, and as far as I know, none of the neighbours have ever had a letter from her.

It changed John. He stayed out of any kind of trouble after that. In fact, he took to religion in a big way. Right now and for the past few years he's been song leader at the evangelical picnics at Canyon Creek.

The rain's stopped. Take your coffee with you. We can sit on the porch where it's cooler. Sure, take your notebook too. If I talk too fast, you just tell me. I'm not used to talking to people. When someone like you comes by and I get feeling easy, I kind of run off at the mouth in twenty different directions . . .

* * *

That long row of buildings there — that was Sid Malan's place before he left.

Everybody reckoned on Sid Malan coming back to her. They reckoned for — well, twenty years at least, according to what my mama remembered.

Sid's wife, Minerva, still lives just across from where the road turns north, on the same land they farmed in the beginning. She farms different than we do. With us it's wheat and barley on the better land, and what's too stony for putting a plough into we turn into potato fields. But Minerva's been putting up long rows of buildings all over her place until it looks like a village all to itself. She turned her place into a chicken ranch, and making good money at it. Not that it makes her laugh any easier, but she's fat and getting fatter all the time, and that's a change.

She put up an electricity line to her place, and last few years she's given up seeding her fields. Says it's cheaper for her to buy grain from us to feed her chickens. I even got a week of work last summer helping her build a new slaughter house and freezer. Now she can hold her slaughtered chickens fresh into the winter, when she gets a better price for them. Now that's good — that's using brains. But it's not the sort of thing would have kept Sid married to her. From all the stories I've heard about Sid, that new slaughterhouse would've ended him.

Sid was a tiny fellow. Never grew any taller than a school-boy.

"But his gab would make you forget the time of day!" my mama often said. "When he stood around talking to you, you'd swear that you heard flutterings like the whole sky was full of birds!"

Before he married, he already owned the land Minerva's been building on. Mind, the place was no farm. I've heard my old man tell there was nothing except a house with a railed-in porch and a woodshed in front. All the rest of his acreage was brush and wild grass. Not even a garden.

"Nice to see the flowers in spring, like the Lord poured a bucket of gold over my place!" was Sid's reply when they got on to him for letting his place go wild.

Back in those days, Sid Malan made his living trading horses and selling second-hand machinery. He was liked, listened to, and jollied around with. And he always had the right price on an old cream separator, used set of harness, or even a bent old garden hoe, if you were looking around for a cream separator, set of harness or garden hoe.

My mama and some of the other women were pushing him to marriage. They had to have something nice to do besides live and work. Today the women have church auxiliaries and home and school clubs. But during the tougher times, it was about all they could do to knit a sweater or marry somebody off.

"Wait! I'll marry! But first I've got to ripen and sweeten some!" Sid would wink at the women and they'd laugh and bounce around and get even more worked up over Sid remaining single for so long.

Then he took up with Minerva, and they began to wonder. She was from around here, which was something.

But she was twice the size of Sid to begin with and her face had that rough and sour look which she still has. She wasn't the tidiest person. Sid was always dressed in a clean shirt and a bit of suit, while she wore and slept a dress to death, and it showed all the damages.

When they married, Minerva put her foot down on Sid's huckstering. She took over a rusty plough Sid had already found a buyer for, and began breaking the land. The first year of their marriage she'd turned over the best soil on the farm and seeded in a good stand of barley. Maybe something in Sid was going under, but everybody figured it was a good thing after all, for Minerva showed she was a woman of the land.

Sid still did horse-trading and machinery selling on the side, but before that first crop was harvested, she had him pulled into the farm. Like she had him help her build a fence around the property. As my old man used to say:

"For weeks you'd see them — Sid squatting close to the ground, his sleeves rolled up, holding steady a stool on which she stood as she hammered down the posts, using a twenty-pound hammer and a wood-chopper's stroke!"

' "Give it a good whop for me, Minerva, me darlin'!" Sid would egg her on. When she really got sluggin', he'd start to sing —

> "On the farm in the morning,
> Many birds awake;
> Over fields and lawning,
> The sweetest music make —
> Chirreep! Chirreep! Chirreep!" '

In those days Sid used to buckboard the ten or fifteen miles into town like everyone else. There were a few cars around even then, but they were expensive and a little scarey to own, since the cop in town liked horses and was even down on a kid with a bike who could make a horse bolt. Most people, my parents among them, found the speed of walking just about right. Any more speed would get you there faster, and what would you do when you got there? But Minerva was different.

She saw her first car parked by the beer parlour in town. She shook it to test its strength.

"We got to have one!" she said to Sid, who was shrinking away with surprise and fear.

And before the summer was out, Sid did some lively trading in almost useless hay-mowers and bought a battered, 1930 Chevrolet for her. Now about every second Saturday my father would have enough heavy produce to take to town to make it worth driving his team and wagon in. But on odd Saturdays he'd only have a crate of eggs to deliver, so he'd go in with a neighbour who was also travelling light. When Sid got the car, he began going over to Sid's.

"I'd no sooner reach his yard," my old man would say, "and Sid would appear with a clean rag and go over this car of his. He'd wipe the dust from the windshield first. Then he'd wipe the headlamps. After that he'd open all the doors so the car looked like a rooster after a dog had worked it over, and he'd clean the seats. He'd wipe the steering wheel an' the gearshift stick. And then he'd give the panel a dusting."

Minerva drove the car with my father sitting beside her. Sid sat in back with only the top of his head showing through the window. He sat in back because the noise and fumes of the motor sickened him with fright.

In their second year of marriage they got some livestock. My mama remembers a golden-haired cow, some pigs and a dozen chickens. She also remembers that Minerva began putting on fat.

Then one day their marriage was all over with.

"It was Friday . . . " was the way my old man always began telling it.

"I think it was Thursday," my mama piped in, just to give him a chance to argue by way of warming up.

"It was Friday — I know it was a Friday because one of the reasons I went to see Sid was to ask for a lift into town the next day. It'd been hot as a torch nozzle that day. I'd been working my summer fallow and had to give up for the heat. So I went over to Sid's to ask for a ride, and also get loan of a wrench I needed to tighten up my equipment."

He'd stop and stab a finger towards his cup — his way of saying to mama he was ready for a refill of tea. When the tea was poured and he'd had a sip to test it, he'd continue with this story.

"As I was saying, I walked into Sid's yard and see him there stripped of the jacket he always wore. He was bent over, his shirt dark with sweat, and he was making a commotion as he tried to corner a large red rooster where the fence around his yard joins the house. Minerva was on the porch, a tiny apron wrapped around her big middle. She'd her hands on her hips and was watching Sid trying to outsmart the rooster.

"When I went up to help, Sid an' the rooster had begun this side-stepping dance with each other — Sid would move a step this way, an' the rooster moved a step that way. When I closed in, the rooster tried to break through my legs, but I pinned him. When I picked him up and give him to Sid, the guy's hands shook and his face had gone white. He gave Minerva a pleading sort of look, his lips moving but no words coming out.

' "All right".'

"That was all she said, and she pointed with her thick finger to the wood block in front of the shed. I'm telling you that Christ God Himself carried His cross easier than Sid carried that rooster to the block. When he got there, he laid the rooster out like he was ready to give him the business. But instead of taking the axe, Sid stood looking at the fields. He stood there an' he stood there, and I could feel the time tearing my skin off a foot a minute, but Sid just stood there, looking . . .

"Then the porch floor creaks and I see Minerva come at him — her mouth hard and dirty, and her eyes on fire. She grabbed the rooster from Sid and give him a shove that damned near put the little man through the fence. Then she picked up the axe and with a quick stroke lopped off that rooster's head. Throwing it in the grass, she turned to Sid. He was looking at her now and talkin' in a soft and furry sounding voice, his eyes filling up with tears.

' "I'll be going now, Minerva, me darling," he said. "I'll be going." '

"She kind of melted a little when she heard that."

' "You don't have to go if you don't wanna," ' she said.

"That was all either of them spoke. He took his jacket off the porch railing an' just walked off without once lookin' back. And she never stopped staring after him. Not once . . ."

* * *

Look — the rain's stopped! The sun will be out before evening!

I was ten, and it was a day like this when 'Whole Damn Cheese' Stiles first came into the community. The road was sticky after the rain. The trees were wet, and the grass smelled of wet lime and slow rot. My old man and I were putting a new roof on the chicken house. We first heard and then saw the old Ford truck growing and twisting down the road towards us like a cow gone blind.

"Who's that?" I asked, looking hard into the sun. A boy at ten can tell most of the cars and trucks in the world just by hearing them, but this one had me buffaloed. My father had a mouthful of nails bristling out. He took the nails out and not taking his eyes off the truck, rolled himself a smoke.

"Don't know," he said. "That truck's old enough to burn straw. Will you look at it!"

It was near our gate now. Its radiator was blowing steam. The box in back of the truck was wired and tied together with rope and each time the machine skidded in the mud the box squealed and leaned over to one side or another, just barely avoiding spilling its load of mattresses and bedding, paper boxes and chests of drawers. Six boys — full grown boys with black beards on their faces, sort of held the load in one place by standing all around the cargo in back of the truck and heaving left when the load shifted to the right. On the very top of the load, rocking like magpies on a windy branch, were two girls, also fully grown. They sat back to back, one facing forward, and the other in the direction from which they'd come.

"They're stopping!" my old man said with alarm and got to his feet.

And sure enough the front wheels of the truck crimped over sharp into our gateway and the whole mess slipped on top of the culvert which crossed the ditch in front of our place. As my father and I came down the chicken-coop roof, a heavy and grey-haired man came out of the truck and walked over to meet us.

"Hullo. Having trouble?" my old man spoke first.

"Yes an' no. Whole damn cheese is boiling. What's the matter, farmer — is this the best road you got hereabout?" He pushed his cap back on his head, stared meanly at my old man and spat out the corner of his mouth. I looked up at my father and saw his ears getting red as he came to a slow boil.

"Same road's been here for twenty years so all kinds of pricks can walk or ride it. You figuring on improving it tomorrow?"

The stranger shrugged with one shoulder.

"No, I won't be changing anything," he said. "But if that's a road, I don't think people should take this whole damn cheese sitting down. That's all."

The two of them stood a couple of yards apart, both

mushing up mud with their shoes. My father's face got friendlier.

"We should've had better roads by now, that's true," he said, looking away quickly. "You aiming to settle?"

"Yeh — sure. Have a look around an' see if there's anything we like. Had a farm in Manville. Lost it. But I'll make out good this time — got me six boys strong as horses now. Say, neighbour you got some cold water I can have for my truck?"

"Sure," my father pointed to the house. "Well's back of there. Help yourself."

We left him to cool his truck and ourselves went back to shingling the roof.

A week or so later we learned they'd picked up a homestead some five miles north of our place. But they never got prosperous. Never made enough to eat and dress properly on. The boys worked hard, but they were a clueless bunch — the kind who pitchfork hay they're standing on. I saw the old man cutting wood once. He was handy but he couldn't be everywhere seeing to things.

"You're going to write all this down? Am I talking too fast? No, it won't matter. I think better when I think slow.

One of the girls married. Not one of the two we saw on the truck, but the one who sat in the cab between 'Whole Damn Cheese' Stiles and his missus. She never had babies though.

The two on the truck knew how to cook and sew, but couldn't get themselves married nohow. Shorty Mack, whose farm begins just across the road, himself not married, thought they should have learned to play mandolins!

Now you take our Shorty — real 'sport' if there ever was a sport. He always dressed in a white shirt with cufflinks, even when he milked cows or did the spring ploughing. He wakes up in the mornings singing and doing bends from the waist down.

"You could hoe a garden with the strength you use up

doing that!" my father used to holler at him. And Shorty
Mack would holler back:

"It takes a good body to house a happy mind!"

I don't think Shorty had two coins to rub together, but
on Sundays he walked with a cane in his hand, and wore a
hat always brushed slick with the brim turned down in
front and bent up at the back. Once my old man and I
stood leaning on the gate, watching Shorty lead a cow to
market.

Shorty didn't have enough money to buy a rope, so he
led his cow by four neckties tied end to end and looped
around the cow's neck. As he led the cow past he looked
straight into my father's eyes. He twisted his head to look
back even when he was past our gate and some distance
down the road. My old man stood like he was a statue made
of stone. He didn't laugh. Didn't even smile.

I've seen days made for fun. And I've seen days and
people over which you've got to weep.

People like Mary and Pete Ruptash. They'd been married fifteen years before they had a kid — a girl with one
missing arm. Pete had built a playroom ten years earlier
for her coming. The playroom had wallpaper with rabbits
on it, a small crib, rocking toys and a little desk with a
chair. And then this baby came.

It had learned to walk and was able to say "Mama, I
busy," and "da-da" when it caught diptheria and died.
Pete had to beat his wife with his fists to take the kid away
so he could bury it.

My first teacher in school was Mr. McFarland, who was
short of breath, and had a moustache which he combed
when he thought nobody was watching. At school picnics
he shook hands with the women and hugged the men up
tight.

"It's funny, but his cheek smells — of lavender," my old
man said after he'd been hugged.

"I was . . . an infantryman in . . . the British Army!"

22

These are among the first words I remember him saying when I began school. I kept dropping my pencil one afternoon and it kept getting under his skin. Then it fell once more, careful though I was, and Mr. McFarland brought me down by suddenly aiming his yardstick at my head and making a 'pow-pow' shooting noise. I was scared — wetting-the-pants scared, for there was hate in his eyes when he did that.

He had a brother named Joseph, who split wood, brought in water and cooked meals for him in the one-roomed teacherage. At recess, Joseph would sometimes come out and play ball with us. He was very tall and always smiled. Once in a while he didn't seem to hear when you talked to him. I kept telling my father about how big Joseph was and how he had to do woman's work. And so when my father got behind with his haying, he asked Joseph to help, and he did. I was in school that day, and when I came home, Joseph was gone.

"Is Joseph finished working?" I asked.

"He's in the barn, brushing down the horses." My old man was down on one knee beside the kitchen door, wiring together a wooden keg that came apart every September. I looked up and saw the large haystack which had taken shape beside the barn.

"Sure is a strong guy, that Joseph!" I said. My father looked up at me.

"First day on a farm any man starts off good. Tomorrow he'll be flat on his back." I was hurt and my father noticed. "Can't expect a man who's never had to work on a farm to be top of the heap. Sure, Joseph's all right."

"Don't you like him?"

"I got nothing against him. And we don't talk enough to argue." He tried to shrug me off.

"He talks sometimes around school."

"He's terrible slow. Men like him end up doing women's work, if they get work at all. I'm sorry, son."

"He can do things, an' he can talk!" I was angry now, wanting to defend Joseph. My father looked at me as if he was trying to explain something I didn't know. He talked slowly to me as he held the pliers in his hand, opening and shutting them with each sentence.

"You seen the lumberman's boots he wears? Well, if he has to put them boots on, lace them and tie the laces, he could do all that quicker than tell you about it."

I saw Joseph opening the barn doors and leaving the barn in that stumbling sort of walk he had. He was very tired, his clothes wet with his sweat. He crossed the yard and left without speaking to us.

"Joseph be back tomorrow?" I asked.

"No, I paid him off."

"But you didn't bring *all* the hay in! Not with a man who doesn't work fast." I argued. My old man was looking at me with eyes that had gone dark and strange.

"I needed a man for one day. It's all I could afford a man for — one day. Any man! So I had to drive Joseph like he's never been driven before!"

"Did you hurt him?" I suddenly saw Joseph as just a big child, trapped in the fields, while my old man worked off every fury on him.

"No. But we had to bring the hay in. He got paid top wages."

Joseph worked at surrounding farms for short periods of time. Most places he got paid off before lunch. War had broken out, and one week he just drifted out of the community and into the army. He came back on furlough once and paid us a visit.

His hair was cut short and he looked good in his nicely pressed army uniform and V-cap. His back had become so straight he might've stood against a tree and his entire length would've touched the trunk. The uniform impressed even my father. He shook Joseph's hand and slapped him

24

across the shoulders. I ran ahead to the house to tell my mother, and she put water on for tea.

After they'd settled in the kitchen and Joseph took his cap off and tucked it in his shoulder flap, my old man tapped his foot with pleasure.

"Well, Joseph — how's it going? Army treating you good?"

"Sure, Mike — treats me real good!" Joseph mumbled and grinned at us all.

My father offered him tobacco and paper and they both rolled and lit up. Leaning against the woodbox next to the stove, I stood watching Joseph and wanting to be a soldier myself. The water sputtered and warmed in the kettle on the stove. Jim came tearing in chasing the cat, once around the kitchen table without even seeing Joseph and out the door into the yard.

"You ain't scared?"

Joseph hadn't heard. I thought it was me my father had spoken to.

"Scared of what?" I asked. My father looked up at me and his ears began turning red. My mother saw and pushed me gently to the door.

"Bring some wood from the shed!" she said quietly. I moved as far as the door, but didn't go out.

"You ain't scared, are you, Joseph?"

"Scared of what?" Joseph woke up, surprised.

"The army. Fightin' — you know, guns pointed at you! Attacks! Getting hurt — maybe even dying!"

Joseph took a deep drag on his cigarette and smiled stupidly.

"I don't aim to — to do no fighting!"

"Then what in hell are you doing enlisting?" My old man suddenly turned sharp with anger. Joseph squirmed.

"Why not? Everything's . . . taken care of. One guy tells you when to get up. Another guy says when you go to sleep . . . An' they feed you good, Mike! Grapefruit juice for breakfast — ya! A glass, this big — for breakfast! Jesus! I never tasted no grapefruit juice before!"

With his brother at war, Mr. McFarland also enlisted and was given a posting guarding potato stores for the Defence Department somewhere in the south of the province. We figured with war ending they'd both come back, but they didn't.

And the years sort of whistle by, but in summer all of us boys went swimming Sunday afternoons where the creek joins the river. There was nobody to spy on us, so we'd strip naked in the sun and before going in the water would make a game of grabbing for each other's dangles. Then we'd wrestle, one hand over the crotch, and the other fighting like hell, each one defending his manhood joyfully.

The river ran swift and straight there. To cool off, I'd swim for an hour or two in the creek, where the water was still and warm. Then I'd go up on the bank and watch the rougher boys swimming against the river current. Six boys, hollering and panting, swimming like their lives depended on it, swimming half an afternoon to gain a yard against the current! Watching them, I often thought what would an ant make of human stubborness?

If Jim had been there he might've told me, for Jim knew more about ants that way than I did.

* * *

This community is still a last outpost.

Ten miles beyond here the road ends in wilderness. If you go another fifty miles past that, you're in muskeg that would swallow you up live in summer. And they say that much further north of that begins the tundra.

There was a lot of trapping carried on here when the Hudson's Bay Company was doing big business in furs. A few trappers still pass through going south in spring and north with freeze-up in October. Whichever way they go, the poor devils are loaded right down. Coming off the trapline in spring, they bring their pelts into town for sale. In the fall, they have to carry all their winter provisions in one load.

Now look at how big this house is — and I'm the only one here now. But when he was building, my old man planned on a big family. A spell of sickness and then the depression years, and after that the real truth that this land takes almost as much as it gives in return — well, he had a big house on his hands and a lot of silly dreams that were already dying when Jim and I were born.

Yet others made use of the house. Word got around among the trappers, and ever since I can remember they made this house an overnight stop before going on. The trappers were a queer bunch. There was one called Weasel Jack, who never said a word. He used to sit on the floor over in that corner and never blink his eyes for watching my folks and us kids. But our favourite among them all was Dan Jacobs!

Dan was skinny as a rail. But to get through that door he had to bow his head, he was that tall! His skin was dark and parched until he looked like a smoked fish. Except for his eyes — they were bright eyes and clear as water and full of fun. He didn't marry, but he used to brag that between the Pelican Rapids and the Arctic Circle he'd fathered forty-two children, most of them on Indian and half-breed women. Except one, a school-teacher in a fishing village who'd burned all the textbooks in her school and was teaching children about a world where there was no more war. The woman's name was Anita, and she was Swedish or Norwegian — Dan wasn't sure which. My father took a strong interest in her, and what Dan had to say about her.

"She sounds like the kind of woman you should marry," he said to Dan.

"She'd make a good wife, yes. But she won't have me.

27

Takes great care of the kids — won't let me help her at all, but this school and the kids there are her life."

"Do the people like her?"

"There ain't a person in that village who wouldn't show you the road out if you said a bad thing about her. They love her — especially the kids she teaches!"

We never got to meet Anita, although she flew out to the city once a year, and one summer Dan told us she'd gone up north by motor-boat, using our river to reach the lake where her village and school is.

Dan knew each of his forty-two kids by name, and carried cartons of chocolate bars for when he would visit them with Christmas gifts that he delivered between the first of December and the end of February. I've seen him sit at this table, an open scribbler in front of him and a chunk of pencil in his hand, writing down what medicines cured colic and sore chests, and my mother talking on and on about the times Jim and I had this and that, and how she made us well.

Now here's something I never got straightened out in my head — my mother's liking for Dan. To her divorce or re-marriage was a real crime. The love of one man for more than one woman was a sin that would put anyone doing this into hell for ever and a day. I've seen her get sore at one of the dances at Anderson's Hall when she saw a man dancing with a neighbour's wife.

But forty-two kids or not, she liked big Dan and washed his shawl and cap for him when he came. She mended his socks after she'd washed and dried them in front of the stove. But he'd never allow his shirt to be washed. It wasn't really a shirt — just a burlap sack turned upside down with openings cut out for the neck and arms.

"Never touch this, Josie!" Dan would warn her. "Or the fleas will come at you and kill you!"

I guess his clothes made one big flea-nest. I've sat up nights watching him open the door of that heater there, with the fire burning so you had to put your hands over your eyes to look in. He'd strip off his shirt and stand naked to the waist. Half-naked like that he didn't seem thin any more. He looked like a man must've looked when he lived in caves, his muscles jumping on his arms and back with every turn and move he made. Dan would flap his burlap shirt in front of the fire. As the fleas burst with a clicking sound in front of the heat, he would laugh.

"Listen to that! Will you listen to that!" he'd whoop and stamp his feet with joy. "Can you hear them buggers sizzle!"

I was afraid of going outside on the nights big Dan stayed over with us. I still feel ashamed and guilty for getting up on a chair and making water through my window into the snow outside. But Don's dogs were outside, howling, snarling and chewing on their leashes which were tied to our garden fence. Dan had pulled the covered toboggan into the middle of the yard out of possible reach of his dogs, but they kept snarling and pawing snow and dirt to get at it.

"They're wild sons of bitches — tear anything apart. Even a block of wood," Dan would say as he went in among them, a length of chain in his hand.

There was the look of killers and scavengers about his dogs. Frozen eared, with yellow, rheumatic eyes and long fangs off which the dark gums had shrunk from sucking icy air on the long, hard winter trap lines.

You know, a man gets to look like that if he lives half-wild long enough. Last time Dan Jacobs was through was about five years back, and I couldn't help feeling that big Dan was carrying a wolf upon his back.

What else do you want to hear — our hatreds! Small hatreds and big ones, like the hatred of Timothy Callaghan for his ox, Bernard. Timothy had eleven or twelve kids — can't remember for certain as there were two that died, but some got born after. To dress up these kids and feed them, Timothy had to work hell out of some ten acres of ground, half of it as stony as the church wall. He could never save enough to buy himself a horse or tractor, so the work of clearing and cultivating and hauling in wood in winter was the job of Bernard.

The ox was slow, lazy, stubborn. When Timothy had to work fastest to keep his soil from drying before the first seed was planted, Bernard would grunt like he was getting sick and start limping. Sometimes he'd lie down in full harness, digging his horn into the ground, turning up his eyes and making like he was dead.

When I was younger, I used to watch Timothy from a distance — watched him lose his temper so completely that he'd take off his cap and beat the ox around the face until all the stuffing in the cloth cap came out. I've also seen him kick the ox, taking a run with each kick. I've seen him work over Bernard's backside with a willow switch, as well as a four-foot alder club. Timothy cursed the ox, and once I saw him get down on his knees and plead with him, while in the trees all around the early summer birds sang, and that was the worst time of all.

I think Timothy cried then, and told the ox everything — how he hated to live and how terrible was the work that had to be done each day.

Then one day Timothy Callaghan came to our place, running and bareheaded, his eyes bulging out of his head.

"It's the devil! He's in that ox of mine!" he shouted. "I've seen the devil in his eyes. He was laughing, teasing me to kill him! One day — one day, I will, and God help me!"

It was talk — only talk. Timothy and the ox were tied together until one or the other died naturally. Sure, they hated each other, but they also needed each other so they could carry on living and eating.

You want to see them? I'll take you over in the morning. Timothy and the ox are both grey now, and kind of too weak to do heavy work any longer. But they still hate, and maybe that's what keeps them living now. What else they got to live for?

Bernard is an ox, and Timothy's family broke up and left him.

* * *

The summer I was nine, Jim had gone to camp and my father was in hospital having an ulcer taken out of his stomach. It's a funny age, nine. It's like you suddenly hurt all over with all the stuff that's baby being torn away from you, and you know you'll never heal proper, which makes you all empty and sad inside. It's also a time when some morning you lift your head from the pillow and everything around you is singing and laughing with a new and stronger music!

See the farmhouse with the green roof over here? That's the Bayrack farm.

The summer I turned nine, Helen Bayrack turned eighteen, and that made such a change. She turned eighteen and she wasn't married, and I was told by my mother:

"I want you to call Helen "Miss Bayrack" now. If I hear any more of this 'doom-doom' nonsense, you'll get a swat across the ears!"

I always called her 'doom-doom'. Used to shout it after her when she came past on her way to the store or on Saturday evenings, her hair all curled, as she walked to the dance at Anderson's Hall. I called her 'doom-doom' because of the way she sang. She liked to sing, but she couldn't remember words to songs she liked. So when she forgot words, she kept right on singing 'doom-doom-doom-doom'. She didn't mind me calling her that name. She liked it. But the summer I was nine and she came eighteen, it seemed to matter.

My mother didn't say it, but somehow I felt she was worried for a girl turned eighteen and not married. And

31

when I got this planted in my mind, I figured I'd marry her myself if nobody else would. I didn't tell Helen Bayrack how I felt because I didn't want to make her think I was soft on her.

She was a beautiful girl. I say this now, for then she was only a girl I liked. Her hair was long and black, and hung down her neck in two thick braids. Her teeth were even and very white. And her skin was tanned deep to the colour of cinnamon from working outside in the sun and wind.

We played together a lot that summer. I teased her and she chased me. When she caught me, she'd put me over the highest branch of the nearest tree and leave me there to hang.

"Hey! Let me down!" I'd holler if she pretended she was walking away and I wasn't sure if she was really pretending or if she meant it.

"You still think I look like a goose?" she'd ask, holding her arms folded in front of her like she had all the time in the world.

"No — heck! You're nice!" I'd swear in a panic, because by now my arms were getting numb from holding on to the branch and the ground was too far down to let go. She'd take me down and laugh.

"You're sure some hero. A grasshopper could jump higher. But did *you* ever shout!"

"You — doom-doom!" I spat at her when my feet touched solid ground. "I hate you!"

I ran then, turning only once to shout over my shoulder. "You look like a goose!"

Then I am standing by our gate, whittling a birch whistle and she goes by on the way to the store, slowing down as she passes me and looking at me with her head turned under and sideways. She is changing. She no longer wears jeans, but is now wearing a blue dress. There are shoes on her feet. I don't know what to say, for I haven't any shoes and the pants I wear are patched at the knees and backside — and that's the difference as I see it then between us.

"Hello, short-stuff!" she says and smiles in a way that cuts into my heart.

I can no longer stand looking at her. I am mad at her for dressing that way. For looking like I'd never seen her before. She is walking away from me. Further and further away. I try to keep my eyes on my whittling, but my hands tremble and I throw down the knife and the piece of wood and run.

I know she has stopped and is looking after me, and I know she is sorry. But I could not return, for now she was Miss Bayrack, and she was eighteen and wanting to marry, and that was the world between us!

On other days, I tried to tell her.

Like I tried to tell her when John Zaharchuk began to court her. He looked terrible, with his dark blue chin gleaming in the sun and the hair of his chest creeping up and over the collar of his shirt. He rode his bicycle when he went to see her.

"Hullo!" he shouted and waved to my father. Then he saw me.

"Hullo, boy!"

My old man waved back, but I wouldn't even look at him. He'd never spoken to us before, and now he spoke, because we were neighbours of Helen's, no other reason. One day he even got off his bicycle and stood talking to my father. He left his bicycle on the road and climbed over the fence to where my father hoed between the cabbage rows. As they talked I slipped away from the garden and out on the road. I let the air out of his tires and they looked up when they heard the hissing. John Zaharchuk picked up a stone and threw it at me. His aim was bad.

"Why don't you kill me? Come on!" I screamed at him, wanting to die standing between him and Helen.

"Come here!" my father called. When I came, he pulled

down my pants and spanked me with a bare hand until he was out of breath. Hanging over my old man's knee I saw an upside-down world in which John Zaharchuk was moving along an upside-down road, pushing an upside-down bicycle with flat tires. He was laughing. I could hear him laughing. That was how I tried to tell her, but she didn't hear me. I felt she had stopped listening.

Another day she picked wild strawberries along the fence where her farm and this one joined. I hid behind the stone-pile and made sounds to her, like those of a pheasant with a broken wing, but she didn't even look up. I cawed like a cow and whistled like an evening lark. But she was where she was, bowed to the ground picking wild strawberries. I crawled away from her and went home, hurting inside like I was going to die.

Soon John Zaharchuk was cycling to her every second day — and once on Saturday and again on Sunday. I watched from behind the barn, not being able to take my eyes away from him for hatred. What kind of a man was it would leave work to ride to a woman? She would starve to death if she married him.

Now there was an idea that pleased me! Helen Bayrack starving to death, no longer able to raise her head with hunger. Running her dry mouth over the stones and boards on which she lay, searching for a crust — and then I coming to see her, bringing a bowl of cooked oatmeal and milk! There beside her was John Zaharchuk. When I came in he tried to grab the bowl and milk with greed.

"Food! Thank God for you, boy! Give me food!" he pleaded. But with the heel of my foot against his cheek I pushed him down and kicked him. Then I lifted Helen in my arms and fed her. Quickly, she became strong again. And then she was up on her feet, running out with me and after me. We played in the sunlight, and I called her 'doom-doom' again and said she was like a goose. She chased me for it and made me apologize.

34

Helen's mother came to see my mother one afternoon and I heard her say, "That Zaharchuk is a good man. He will make a good husband for my Helen."

I ran out of the house and back of the barn. There I picked up a stick and beat it to pieces against the log wall.

That week the stranger came.

He was one of those guys who'd lived and worked all his life in town. McQuire was his name. Philip McQuire. He was bald and fat, and old enough to be Helen's father. He talked loud and drove a small car. And he smelled of shaving lotion and pipe tobacco.

Once my mother sent me to Helen's place to ask for some pickling salt. McQuire drove up behind me, and stopped to offer me a ride. He laughed a lot when I got in the car, and he called me 'Buster'.

When he turned the car into Helen's place, I asked him, "What for you coming here?"

"Well now, Buster — it's not easy to give you an answer to 'What for you coming here?' You get a little older and along will come a pretty girl — and you'll know. Or maybe you've got yourself a little girl friend now, you little bugger!" He laughed and poked me in the ribs with an elbow. We got out of the car and I ran ahead to tell them he'd come.

He was a plumber, which meant he had money and so was a cut above us farmers. Helen's folk were Ukrainian, and McQuire learned very soon to say 'dobra, dobra!' to anything they told him, and this went over very big.

"Understand me," Helen's father said in the grocery store one Saturday evening, his chest stuck out and his eyes shining. "Understand me please when I say this McQuire is the man for my girl! He's a plumber — a skilled man, not like our farm boys. He's got gas, water and power — important people come to see this McQuire of ours, and they call him "Mister". Even the mayor of the town calls him "Mister"! Now what do you think of that?"

The group sitting around the store said nothing. But you could see who the Ukrainians were, because they were all scratching their head in about the same places. Old man Bayrack saw this, and said to them:

"This McQuire is not like the rest of *them*! He speaks our language. He eats what we eat. Last Sunday he tasted creamed chicken and dumplings my wife made just for him and he said, 'Dobra, missus, dobra!' Now what do you think of that?" He took a deep breath, straightening his back proudly and half-closing his eyes as he went on to say, "I tell you my grandchildren will carry the name of McQuire, but they shall speak our language!"

The Ukrainians stopped scratching and looked up at him. They believed him. You could feel the change in the air of the store, and there was nothing more anyone could say.

John Zaharchuk cursed and swore there was nothing for him but the rope when he heard of this McQuire. For a while he continued visiting the Bayrack home, on the days McQuire did not call.

My mother asked Helen's mother why Zaharchuk kept courting when it was plain McQuire was the man Helen would marry.

"To finish eating the cookies I baked for our Philip the day before!" Helen's mother said angrily.

There is a saying here that a courtship is like milk. Taken fresh it gives good health and long life. But allowed to grow old, it sours. So on the first Sunday when the hay was in and no other work was pressing, Helen's people invited the neighbours for a dinner at which Helen's engagement would be announced to the world.

"If only your father was well enough to come. He never missed such a dinner before!" my mother griped as she fixed up the suspenders on the clean pants I would have to wear. I hated the way these pants smelled of P and G soap and mothballs. We used mothballs to kill potato beetles, and the smell of mothballs came to mean insect death to me. But I never got around to telling her all this, because as she was doing up the last button, McQuire arrived, hooting his car horn in the yard. He had driven over to get us.

The Bayrack house was small, hot and humming with flies who came after the sweet-smelling iced cakes.

"Here — make yourself useful, or they'll mistake you for a stool and put a glass on your head!" Helen's mother gave me a whisk of willow branches, with which to shoo out the flies through the open door and windows. From the parlour came sounds of shouting, laughter and shuffling feet. McQuire was in there, offering whisky to the men. He'd been drinking before he came to our place, because driving over he kept steering from one edge of the road to the other, and my mother was so nervous she grabbed my knee and held on tightly all the way.

"Dobra! Dobra!" He kept hooting. "Die Bosheh — drink! God provides, and all that jazz!"

I looked around for Helen among the women in the kitchen. She wasn't there. My mother was also looking for her.

"Such a shy girl you've never seen — she's gone into the barn to think things over. Silly, silly girl! Why when I was her age and in this situation I was so cock-sure . . ."

"Paraska — the boy!" One of the women cut in and pointed at me. Helen's mother looked up from the turkey she was carving, saw me, and the giggle died on her face. Then she blushed. But some woman in back by the stove cackled a dirty laugh and everybody seemed ashamed because of me.

I stopped swishing and the flies came back into the kitchen like a dark cloud. I wanted to leave and find her. But what could I say to her when I did see her? She was eighteen and about to be married, and I was somebody called 'short-stuff' from down the road. I didn't matter and

37

there could be no friendship left for us. I still had an anger ache in me, but I wasn't sure who I was angry with.

Then I looked up and she was standing in the doorway!

"Oh, my child!" Her mother threw the meat knife to the floor and moved over to hug Helen up. Helen turned her face away, and her cheek was red and hot.

She was more beautiful than ever before, and the anger hurt got very big in me. I couldn't close my mouth as I looked at her, for my breath was choked between my ribs. Her black hair had been brushed so good it rose in deep piles over her head and down her neck. The blue dress she wore gave off a light, like water under the sun. She seemed thinner. She trembled so only I would see, and tears came to her eyes. I looked down at her hands, and saw how much she'd cried, for the knuckles were wet still from rubbing her eyes with them.

"Helen Bayrack, my dobra, dobra! Gimme a chum-chum!" Philip McQuire came roaring out of the parlour, a whisky glass in one hand and the other pushing aside the women in his way. He pushed away Missus Bayrack like she was a sack of potatoes and tried to get both arms around Helen. She moved back and he spilled some whisky over her dress. She yelped with surprise and hurt.

"Hey — dobra, dobra! Die Boshch!" McQuire turned quickly and sprayed the guests with a long sweep of the hand in which he held his whisky glass. The crowd moved back and McQuire grinned. His eyes now swam in thick pools which bulged out of his face and threatened to burst and pour out of his head.

Helen's mother began to bawl loud. I looked around to see if my mother would go home. The people were crowded near the stove, at the back of the room by this time. They seemed mixed-up, sad — something had gone wrong and the laughter was gone from them. Then a stone came flying through the open door. It barely missed McQuire's

head and fell to the floor with a wallop, then rolled under
the stove.

Helen's mother stopped bawling and bent down to look
under the stove after it. Helen's father hoisted his trousers
like he meant business and stepped outside.

"What you want here? You got no business here! Go
home — get lost!" He came back in and closed the door
behind him.

"Who's there?" Helen's mother asked.

"It's that John Zaharchuk, crazy fool!"

"Is he gone for sure?"

"Naw. But he'll go. What's the matter? He's got no
summer fallow to plough or something, the crazy fool?"
Helen's father stuck out his chin and looked over the heads
of everybody in the room.

"His whole farm is gone to pigweed. Besides, he's not the
man! Here's the man!" He pointed to McQuire.

"He's got gas, water and power! And important people
call him Mister — even the mayor! Now that's really something, if you ask me!"

"Dobra! Dobra!" McQuire hooted, letting go of Helen
and bending over with laughter. Then he threw his glass on
the floor and grabbed Helen's father and pulled him fast to
where he stood. He puckered and kissed Helen's father
loudly on the ear. Helen lifted her hand to her eyes and
began to cry.

Now the guests came alive again. They began moving
around, laughing, congratulating.

"It is true what he says — important people call him
Mister all right — live long!"

There was a crash, a scream, and everybody stood silent
again, looking at one another. The door was split down the
middle, with the blade of the wood-chopping axe coming
through into the room.

"Look!" Helen's mother pointed to the axe blade. "He
could've killed someone!"

39

"Come out and fight! I'll make mush of the town bum!" John Zaharchuk shouted in a thick voice through the window.

"Hey! Hey!" Helen's father walked over to the door and threw it open, but stayed back in the kitchen, only poking his head around the frame this time. "I said get out of here — go home! Helen is spoken for — you've no business here!"

"I want to kill the fat town-boy!" Zaharchuk was in the doorway now, frothing at the mouth and his shirt opened to the belt. His hair-matted chest jumped each time he gasped for air.

"I'll show him who gets her! I'll fight him with bare hands or an axe, whichever way he wants! Or race him on a horse to see who rides better! Or maybe he wants to show me how much man is still left in him — I'll dig a ditch with him. We'll dig from now until sundown, and who digs farther and deeper gets Helen! Okay?"

Helen's mother marched up to him and putting both hands on his chest, gave him a push. "Go away — pshaw!"

She didn't move John Zaharchuk an inch. He didn't even see her, and she walked back to the stove as if she didn't know what to do next. Zaharchuk was staring at McQuire, who was wiping the dribble off the sides of his mouth with his thumb.

"Wait! If he wants a contest, I'll give him a contest!" McQuire said drunkenly, not looking at Zaharchuk at all, but taking away the glass from Helen's father and peering around for the bottle. Zaharchuk laughed hard.

"Don't be crazy, Philip!" Helen's father started to argue. "You don't have to do it."

"You — farm boy!" Suddenly McQuire was looking straight at Zaharchuk, and his voice became strong and firm. "Those things you want to try me for — that's out. I don't fight or ride horses. Last time I dug a hole in the ground was to bury a dead budgie bird! It's like me saying

40

to you, race you to see who can thread more pipe in half an hour. I'd have a hundred feet of pipe tied up before you'd figure out what to do with the die!''

John Zaharchuk wasn't laughing any more. He was straining to understand what McQuire was saying and what he should do about it. But McQuire had more to say.

"Let's do something fair and square to us both. Let's see who can drink five pounds of melted butter first!''

"W . . . What!" Zaharchuk's blue chin was quivering with surprise.

"First guy who drinks five pounds of melted butter gets Helen. Okay?'' McQuire walked away and came out of the parlour with his bottle. He poured himself a stiff drink and took it down with one swallow.

"Okay — farm boy?''

"Okay!" John Zaharchuk was suspicious as a cat, but there was no way out for him no more.

"That settles it — okay everybody — first we win Helen, then we have fun!" McQuire was refilling the men's glasses. Someone even gave Zaharchuk a glass, but he stood near the door and would not drink. The women set about melting the butter, which Helen's father brought in cold and hard from the well where it was kept from going rancid. As the butter crackled and sputtered in two pitchers on the stove, the men moved slowly to the parlour. Even Zaharchuk went in at the end, while the women returned to preparing the meal as if nothing unusual was happening.

"I bet a dollar on Zaharchuk! He's built bigger than you, Philip!'' a man shouted from the parlour, and there was laughter.

"I bet two dollars on Philip. It took some stretching to get a gut that big!" Again there was laughter.

"Men! Dogs, that's what they are! Give a man a drink of whisky and a chance to make some money and he'd sell his own mother!" Helen's mother complained, but she was really happy, because her house was at peace again.

41

I was alone and forgotten, and no one even remembered I was supposed to keep the flies away. I turned and saw Helen, sitting on a bench in a dark corner of the room, looking at me. Her eyes were large and full of pain and laughter, like those of a small girl who bangs her toe on a sharp stone just when she's having one heck of a good time playing a game.

"Doom-doom."

I formed the words with my lips. Then I forgot all the women around me and rushed to her, falling to my knees before my beautiful friend. She reached down, and putting her cool hands under my chin, lifted me up.

"Hello, short-stuff! You're a bad boy to run away from me like this!" she said, and I covered my face with my hands so she wouldn't see my happiness and shame coming all at once.

I stayed at her side as the contest took place. When Zaharchuk and McQuire stripped to their trousers and reached for their pitchers, I knew this was the end — the very end of white skies and days without hours for me. My father was in hospital, my mother worried and my brother was away. It was a sin to whittle and play when the whole world was worried and busy.

They lifted the pitchers to their lips, waiting for Helen's father to give the signal to begin, and I started to chirp like a bird — making cries like a pheasant with a crushed wing and all the other pheasants flown and none to help. Then I cawed like a crow, and whistled the gentle cry of the evening lark. My hand hurt from where Helen caught it and squeezed it in hers.

I trilled and warbled; the kildeer — the twitter of an oriole sitting on its nest with its face to the wind — and she squeezed and she squeezed until I cried aloud with this and other pains.

"Dobra!"

Shouted McQuire, and he turned his empty pitcher up-side down first. And there was a cheer.

Helen Bayrack released my hand, for she was eighteen again, and she had a man to go to.

* * *

I am thinking — trying my damnedest to remember the name of the man who counts. Andrew — Andrew some-thing or other. It was a Polish name. He was from Krakow, and the way he told it in the old days he made out like he owned the city.

"I wore white gloves, and the nobility thought I was one of them and doffed their hats to me." I still remember him saying when he was able to speak. Now he has fallen so with his silences I can't even remember his name — strange.

You can see him if you like. He's around, from the moment the sun rises and he comes out of his house, until night falls and the last turkey has found a perch on the rigs, thin and wild-looking Andrew is around counting on his fingers. Each time he says a number, he stabs the air with his arms.

He's been counting — what? Fifteen years, twenty — I don't know. He's up to four now, which is an improvement, because only a year ago he couldn't get up to the number three twice in one day.

If you're in town tomorrow, call in to the Chinese cafe for a coffee and you'll see Andrew there. Tomorrow is Saturday, market day in these parts. Andrew's always in town on Saturday. He goes into the Chinese cafe and sits at the table nearest the door. It makes no difference if somebody is already sitting at this table. He'll sit down anyway. But we know him here, and feel sorry for the poor bugger. I always buy him a coffee and a chunk of raisin pie. He's crazy about raisin pie — so crazy that if you ever eat with him he'll put you off eating for the rest of the day!

43

Nobody talks to him. But it doesn't matter, even if he butts in on you while you're talking to someone else. It doesn't matter.

"One . . . two . . . two . . . . One . . . . two . . . two . . . . THREE!"

With that he'll wallop the table with his fist so hard all the dishes jump a foot, because he's made it again! Like I say, you get to feel sorry for the poor bugger.

My old man knew him well from way back before Jim or I were born. He tells that Andrew did some farming in those days. Used to fight a lot too. You wouldn't guess it to see him now, because he doesn't stand taller than five feet and his weight is somewhere about . . . oh, a hundred and ten pounds at most.

"Andrew was a mean sonofagun when he got sore," my old man used to say.

"How could he fight? There isn't much man to him?"

"Hudson's Bay rules, boy. Andrew fought by Hudson's Bay rules!"

"What's Hudson's Bay rules?"

"Dirty rules — meanest fighting a man can do. Biting, scratching, kicking, fingers-in-the-eye and knee-in-the-crotch sort of thing. If you was to bundle all the dirty, sneaky tricks into one man, that man would be Andrew!" my father said with an angry grunt.

"He must've lost some fights!"

"Some, but not many." My old man tried to explain a fact of life very slowly so I'd understand. ' "If a guy got tangled with Andrew he'd do as well to lose. Because if he roughed Andrew up fair and square, that pint-sized little bugger would get his own back by clubbing from behind whoever had beat him."

"Then maybe he's lucky he's in the shape he is now. If he'd stayed strong and fighting, by now somebody would've killed him " I said, feeling wise as hell. My old man sort of looked at me and through me.

"You figure that would've been worse than what Andrew's got now?" he asked, then answered himself, "Maybe it would at that."

Andrew got the way he is by hoeing a carrot patch on a hot day and not wearing a hat on his head. His head got so hot from the sun he passed out. When they found him and poured enough cold water on him to bring him around, he'd lost most of his memory and speech. He didn't know his name, although he seemed to have no trouble finding where he lived. The municipality voted him a small tobacco pension and he's been counting up to four since.

There are others half-in and half-out of life as life might be. Like Stanley, our horse-trader. He comes through every August selling horses which he leads tied to one long rope back of his wagon. When you see him leading eight or ten horses down the road that way you'd almost expect to hear a guitar playing and someone singing about the wind and the long, lonesome road, just like they do in the movies!

Stanley was short-sighted, so much so that when two horses on the tail end of eight broke free, he drove twelve miles before he stopped, counted them and learned he'd lost the two. Farmers traded mean stock off on him, throwing in five or ten dollars in conscience money, because some of the horses turned over to Stanley were so mean they would kick or chew a stall to pieces. Anybody else but Stanley would've been killed by these brutes long ago. Yet Stanley didn't know the danger he lived with every day.

With my own eyes I've seen him put up a dozen horses into stalls lining opposite sides of the corridor in our barn. Now our barn is narrow. A horse could kick right across the corridor and into the next stall if he'd a mind to. Like I say, I've seen Stanley walk down that corridor and the horses leaving the floor with their rear legs as they sent out volley after volley of kicks at where they heard him walk. Any one of those kicks should've killed him — but they always missed! He was like Christ Himself walking through the waters!

He never even suspected they were out to get him.

My mother was with me when I saw him walk through all those kicks, and she crossed herself and sat down on the barn-door ramp. After Stanley was gone into the house, I sat down beside her and watched her chew a long piece of straw until she made a little round ball of it in her mouth. She spat it out and got to her feet.

"If those were my horses," she said, looking back into the barn, "I'd lock this barn up, pour two gallons of coal oil around it and set fire to it. There's more evil stabled there tonight than I've seen in a lifetime of living!"

Here — let me warm up some more coffee! How about a can of meat and some bread?

You want to know about love? What can I tell you? Of Nancy Burla? Or Marta? Later, when the sky clears altogether so that I can walk as I tell you, for I must have air and soil under my feel to tell of those loves.

Love could be a cat's tooth, like that one that bit Clem, the blacksmith. He was so honest and good you couldn't really talk to the guy without sounding rougher than you meant to be. If he'd been born five or six hundred years ago, he'd have made it as a saint.

Jim was still around when my old man and I called on Clem, bringing an iron wagon-tire between us for him to shorten. The old man had bought this wagon from some farmer selling out, but when he brought it home, he found the wheels all shrunken. We ended up with more trouble and expense on our hands than a more costly, newer wagon would've cost in the first place.

When we got there, Clem was in the smoke-black smithy. It's still there, about four miles this side of town — you might've seen it when you came up. Clem's clothes were always glued to him with sweat, and his beard and long hair jiggled each time he brought his hammer down on the anvil.

He looked up when we rolled in the tire, and gave us one of those beautiful white-tooth grins only he has.

"Well, men — what can I do for you?"

My old man explained what he wanted done and Clem nodded.

"I'll get on it soon's I have breakfast."

"Breakfast? You mean to say you haven't eaten yet?" My father stared at him. "It's noon already."

"No! Working alone like this, I eat when I get hungry, and I just haven't eaten today." He picked up his hammer and balanced it like it weighed no more than a paint brush. My father was thinking pretty deeply as he looked at Clem.

"No need for a man to be alone," he said. "Clem — you been pounding that anvil on to ten years now. When you going to take a break? Get out and meet people? Do a bit of drinking and rolling around with the girls? This kind of life isn't natural. You're still young and it's not right for a man to work like this!"

Clem was staring at my old man as if what he heard was said in a foreign language.

"I'm happy like this. If I wasn't happy, what could I do? I haven't seen a girl who needs me." He spoke with surprise and something like bitterness in his voice.

"A girl needing you — why a girl that needs you? Don't you need a woman for a wife?" My father leaned back against Clem's tool-bench, ready to argue anything just to keep from having to go home and do work that was endless. I picked up a pair of pliers and pretended to be straightening a bit of copper wire. Clem turned to his anvil, but he seemed worried now.

"I want a woman — true, it bothers me so I can hardly sleep some nights. But a man must give happiness to the woman who needs his help. There is so much unhappiness in this world we live in."

He lowered his head, and again I say he looked like a saint in one of those religious calendars you see in homes

where they got crucifixes hanging on every wall. My old
man coughed one of those rolling 'harrumph' coughs of his
and said, "We'll see about that!"

"What sort of woman would you marry?" he asked
after a while.

"I never really thought it out, but it'd have to be
some girl who needed my help and understanding . . .
an unfortunate girl." Clem looked at my father with
clear, trusting eyes, almost like the eyes Jim had when
he was a kid.

"Aw, come on off the fancy baloney! You know the
difference between a woman and a man — they're built
different — you know that! Talk about women and you've
got to talk about stuff that makes kids — the other's for
the birds!" My old man got quite a kick out of pushing
Clem that way. Clem blushed deep red and gave his anvil a
hard whop with the hammer. He left the hammer lie on the
anvil and turned to my father, but not looking at him any
more.

"Suppose," he began quietly, "suppose I was to see a
young woman — about to be a mother, let's say, and she's
standing on a bridge, wanting to jump over into the river
and end it all."

Clem stuttered now and the colour came up high in his
face.

"I . . . I would run to her. And . . . and carry her away
with me! I would work for her. Make her laugh again and
keep her and her child happy and alive!"

Clem was still talking when my father touched me and
nodded for us to go. We were at our buggy and getting
ready to drive away when Clem came out and called for us
to wait and hear what he had to say.

"Get a woman — a lumberman's whore if you like, and
lock yourself up with her for three days! Then I'll listen to
you!" my old man shouted back and turned our team
homeward. I turned to see Clem holding out his thick

48

arms to us, as in benediction. My father never bothered to look back.

"I'll be back for the tire tomorrow!" he barked over his shoulder.

"Right!" Clem called from a distance now. As we rounded the bend in the road, I could hear his hammer ringing on the anvil again.

Clem did get married to a girl from town.

She wasn't a mother-to-be as you might expect. And she wasn't found on a bridge planning to end her life. She wasn't all that young, but neither was Clem when I think of it.

They met outside the town hotel — Clem walking along minding his business, and she pulling up her dress to show where the policeman arresting her had first grabbed for her — and was this legal? A few men gathered around her, asking to show them again, and the cop laughing into his fist. When she saw she was being led on, she told them all in a high whisky voice to go to hell and leave her alone.

Clem sat through her trial, during which she was charged with disorderly conduct. After she was sentenced, he went over to tell her who he was. Then he paid her fine and took her to the Chinese cafe for supper. And a week later they were married in the magistrate's office.

Clem continued working in his smithy after his marriage, only now he whistled while working, which made all the men and some of the women in the community smile. Curtains appeared in the windows of his shack back of the shed, and for the first time since anyone could remember, he cleared up the junk mouldering around the place and mowed down the grass. This nice life lasted about three weeks. Then she went into town and got herself roaring drunk.

Jim and I were running down the sidewalk, carrying the cream cheque we'd been sent to collect for our mother from the creamery. We were alongside the hotel when the

beer parlour door was thrown open and one of the bar-
tenders pushed Clem's wife outside.

"This is a nice place — quiet farmers, root pickers and
lumberjacks drink here!" he shouted at her. "So don't you
ever come back again!"

Mother came around the corner of the building and tried
to make Jim and me go with her, but the two of us locked
our hands together and pretended we didn't hear or see her.
A crowd was gathering quickly. Then Clem pushed his way
through to her.

"Let's go home," he said quietly. He was worried and
looked up at all of us as if asking us why we stayed and
what we saw that we had to stand open-mouthed. Yet we
stayed.

"Take your goddamned paws off, you queer!" She pushed Clem away. "He never had a woman before! Would you
believe it, the blacksmith never laid with a woman before
me — he didn't know anythin'!"

She wagged her finger under his nose and laughed
viciously. Clem slapped her hand down, and taking hold of
her wrist yanked her through the crowd and around the
corner of the hotel. She was digging her heels down and yel-
ling for him to let her go or she'd put him in jail. By this
time mother got Jim and me by the ears and marched us
away from the hotel.

"Shame on you standing like that watching!" I did feel
ashamed. But when I looked over at Jim, he was grinning
and looking down at his feet.

Clem's smithy stayed shut for a couple of weeks after
that. We came to collect our wagon tire and had to knock
many times on Clem's door. It was finally opened by his
wife, whose face was swollen and bruised.

"What do you want?" she rasped at my old man.

"Is Clem around? I've some repair work to pick up."

"I don't know where he is. Go away!"

She slammed the door shut in our faces. As we walked

past the shop we saw the growing pile of ploughshares and broken rods and pieces of machines brought to be welded and then left for when Clem would re-open.

Jim, my father and I were among the first in the place when Clem did open up. I was surprised at how thin he'd got, and how grey his hair and beard seemed now. Other neighbours started arriving and watching him fire his forge. He picked up his hammer, held it for a moment, then turned to all of us.

"It's all over now. I'll be working again — it's finished. She's gone. The marriage is kaput! She's giving me a divorce . . ." He turned away from us.

"She's giving you a divorce?" my father piped in. "How much is that favour costing you, Clem?"

Clem blew his nose and kept his face turned away from the men in the shed.

"Thirty dollars a month! It's all right — I agreed to that. I'd of given her even more if she'd wanted."

"On top of that, you're paying for the divorce?"

"Yah." Clem nodded.

"You're going to keep paying her until you fall dead at your anvil?" Another man asked this.

"Get out — all of you! How can I work with you blocking out my light? You farmers have nothing to do with your time?" Clem glared at all of us now. He pointed to the door with his hammer and one by one we all drifted out.

Clem got more tired and grey-looking. His eyes became dull and dead, and he never seemed to even wash any more. Anyone could tell he wasn't making the money to pay her, because he was selling out tools from the shop.

Two years after divorcing, she married a shyster selling stocks with get-rich-quick prospects to farmers. By this time the blacksmith shop was stripped down to little more than the forge, anvil and hammer Clem used all the time. He'd even hawked his acetylene welding cart. But even after she re-married, Clem continued to go downhill. I was with my old man the day he stopped before the shed and went roaring off at Clem for splicing a disc axle that didn't hold a damn.

"Look here, Clem!" I heard him argue. "It's none of my business, but I'm not going to bring my work to you no more if you keep paying off that woman of yours and welding axles for me with spit and wire! You can't sell all your equipment for her sake and expect to stay in business! She's married now, and you're still paying for the keep of that pimp of hers and her. Look at you, man! You're still wearing the clothes you bought before your own wedding. And look at your shop — how can you work with what's left? I'm telling you now — either stand up on your feet, or I'm taking my business to the repair shop in town!"

With that my father came stamping out of the smithy, his toothless mouth clamped tight. Clem came out right after him. He was smiling sadly, and brushing his white hair back from his sticky forehead.

"Take your business elsewhere if you wish," he said. "Let her have what happiness God can give her now. Let her have this — I don't care. I can't eat. I can't sleep without her. Soon it will end — soon I will be an old man and it won't matter."

"You damned fool — you're killing yourself! You're killing her! Your money only makes it easier for her to drink and brawl her life away!" My old man was fighting mad now.

"Look neighbour." Clem became sad, far-away. "Stay out of this — do that for me. You don't understand how I feel. My love . . . the way I wish it to be . . ."

Slowly, as if it were the hardest thing he could do that day, he turned his back on us and went back into his shed to work.

* * *

You ever eat honey? Me — I can't eat it.

Mike Sadownik keeps a bee-farm in these parts. He has a large tumour on the back of his neck — big as his fist. He never buttons his shirt all the way up, and he can't push his hat to the back of his head for his lump. I don't know how or why, but I came to think he got this lump from eating honey. I started to think that way as a kid. I've never been able to forget and think different.

I've never been able to eat honey.

When you're born poor, the price of learning a lot and getting away from it is too high. Because you can't do it alone, that's why. Someone has to help, and you can't stop taking once you begin. Jim kept needing more and more help — and we kept paying and paying. Even now there is still so much has to be paid for, and that's the worst thing, because Jim can't put it to use and it's all lost.

Towards the end, he realized how much it cost to make him the great student he was. He wrote one letter to me while he was walking through Hammersmith in London at night. He wrote it against the side of a wall, using a street lamp for light. It was a sad letter. He was a young man who lost one world and never felt at home in another. He said it that way in his letter. I burned the letter. It was mine to read and remember — only mine.

No, Jim did not ride motorcycles. He didn't own one in Canada. He was not the person to enjoy it. I could, if I had one handy, but not Jim. And not at eighty miles an hour on a winding English road like they say. Yes, I think Jim took his life, but don't write that in your story. If my mother should hear of it she would never forgive me for saying so.

I loved him, I hated him — what's the difference now?

I never saw him ploughing fields or walking between the rows of barley, gathering stones in his arms. From the time I remember fields and everything on them, I begin to forget Jim. We walked as kids down some roads together — we

53

even danced once. At times we sat in the Chinese cafe and chewed ice-cream cones. Then he followed his books where they took him and I opened the land. After he'd gone I hated him, because he left me with torn pants and a thin shirt on my back. Yet I'd give it all to him double if he was around now and I could ask him to tell me why a mother leaves her son to look for God. Or why love should hurt so much.

Maybe we're both forever kids — him and me! Maybe all the pain and bleeding never took place — it was all a dream, and my old man will come out of that room there, rubbing the sleep out of his eyes and chewing on his toothless gums. And my mother will show up pretty soon with the milk-buckets full of froth and say if one of us will separate the cream from the milk, she'll put on some rice pudding for supper!

Man, I sure wish my old man was alive! I sure need him now!

She always felt I hated him, but he and I worked together. You work with a man, even if he's your father and you don't see eye to eye with him. He's still your chum as long as you pull the same saw or heave stones off the same field. We worked together that way.

But I was young, and once I tried to shake a weight someone else placed on my neck. I quarrelled, and through the quarrel, I began killing my own father.

"How come Jim's not helping us cut? He's been home from school a week and a half and he's not put down his books and come out to help!" I cut into my old man when we were in the creek hollow, cutting frozen spruce for cordwood. Jim was home for Christmas holidays, but we only saw him at meals. Even then he brought a book down and buried his face in it as he ate. He'd only put on his jacket and go outside when he had to go to the john next to the barn. And when he came back into the house, he never brought an armload of wood with him.

"How come?" I asked. The old man turned to me. He was trying to look angry, but his eyes were sad.

"You leave Jim alone — he's working same's you. Only he's working with his head! You understand that? With his head! There's gonna be some good come out of it — so leave him alone!"

"Why do I have to leave him alone?" I asked biting back the tears, sure that Jim had never been told to leave *me* alone. "He's been in town getting school since he finished grade eight. I never did get to grade eight."

I could see how I was hurting him, and I felt glad of it. I still felt sorry for myself — still tried to keep the tears from coming. Watching him squirm helped me. The old man gripped his axe so tight the knuckles of his hands stood out like white knots in wood.

"Don't ever talk like that, son. I'll make it up to you after Jim's all fixed up. Jim's not as strong or as big as you. But he's smart. Our help now is going to make something of him. Your mama and me are thinking of you. There'll be a farm for you to work for yourself, don't worry . . ."

He spat, and I knew he felt better too.

Maybe you want to see Jim's room? It's behind that door — go ahead. I don't want to go in there. Go ahead, open the door! It hasn't changed in ten years — the same yellow bedspread on the bed. Jim and I chipped in the nickels and dimes we earned on errands to buy that for her for Mother's Day — and you know, she gave it to him before he went away.

"It 's the nicest spread in the house. It belongs on his bed for when he comes home!" she said smiling like a mother.

Look past the lamp and up the wall. See the lousy medal hanging there? Jim got that in school for knowing how to spell, and for something called citizenship. What's this thing, citizenship? You know? Being the good joe all the time? Who decides that?

This is the part of Jim I hated. The hoarding of tin and

paper. A callus on a hand tells its own story. When a bright man speaks, it's the same. I don't like people who take medals as if they had to have it proven to them they were good. And I don't like the people who give out these medals. By giving out a medal they make out like they are better than the best of us. Medals meant a lot to my mother. It gave her something to look up to. And that's yet another reason I hate medals.

Anyway, the lousy thing's up there on the wall. She used to take it down to polish at Christmas and Easter.

The summer Jim was sixteen he came home for a week. The other summers he got work in the school for all the holidays. But this year a new job came up in the library and the person holding it had a week to go before leaving and letting Jim in. So Jim came home. He bought me one of those turtle-neck sweaters — matching one he already had. We didn't say much to one another, but we seemed to be laughing a lot then, and mother was so happy about this that she broke her neck trying to find things for both of us to do together. There wasn't much to do. It was the spell between haying and discing up the summer fallow, so we were all sort of laying around.

There was a dance, and I said to Jim we should go. He agreed. It was over at Anderson's Hall. The same crowd came out, liquored up just as much as every other dance.

About midnight someone lets out a whoop and throws a stick at the lamp. Like always, he missed. Someone else sent an empty beer bottle sailing to where the orchestra was playing on the stage. Sammy Wallis, the long kid who play-. ed the piano, tumbled off his seat before he even saw the bottle coming for his head. The bottle hit the far wall, and Sammy is back on the stool without missing a note of music on his piano. Down on the floor they stopped dancing. A guy figures he knew who threw the bottle, and without a word of warning goes over and punches this sleepy farmer in the kisser. The farmer shakes his head with

surprise, sees the man who hit him, and just as quick hits
him back in the nose. By now the fight has spread. Sammy
has taken his backend off the piano stool with excitement
and is speeding up the music to keep time to the punching,
kicking and cussing going on below him.

The ladies are squealing and backing up against the walls.
A fat lady backed into the stove, knocking it over, bringing
down twelve feet of stovepipe and all with a cloud of soot.
It makes one hell of a noise, and two jokers grab a stovepipe each and start bashing each other across the heads,
making dirty sounds with their lips each time they hit or
get hit.

I catch sight of Jim walking quickly to the door. He
never made it on his own steam. A big fellow fresh from the
lumber-mills catches him, lifts him over his head and throws
him. As aims go, this one was pretty good. Other than clip-
ping an elbow against the door frame, Jim sailed through
that door like it was cut out just for him to be pitched
through. I was tangled with a kid who didn't want to fight,
so I broke off and went after my brother.

Jim was on his feet, his pullover pulled up around his
chest, when I saw him outside. He was brushing dirt off
his pants and face.

"Attaboy, Jim!" I was happy and shook him by the
shoulder, for I was in the heat of the fight and really full of
it.

"You hurt?" I asked, because he was looking around like
he'd lost his directions.

"No. I'm not hurt. Let's go home." And he started to
walk away.

"Go home? You're crazy! Tell you what, Jim," I came
up behind him and caught him by the hand. "Let's you and
me go back and clean up on the smart guy who threw you.
I saw everything — I know who it was! Come on!"

Jim tore his hand out of my grip. He was suddenly so
mad he was trembling all over.

"I'll go home alone!" he snapped at me. "As for you — you go right ahead back into that pigsty and enjoy yourself with those dirty, smelly hogs on a night out! I've had enough of this sort of thing!"

He turned and was gone. I didn't go back into the hall, but followed slowly after him. The music was playing a waltz now, so I knew the fight had ended. Nobody really had that much heart to keep it going any longer. I followed Jim slowly, letting him stay ahead. I was feeling guilty and wondering what was wrong with me — why there was no contact or pride in what Jim felt important, and which I never saw. And why I could never tell him how I felt because he was too far away to hear me now. That was the end of our laughter that summer. Even the two matching pullover sweaters we wore seemed like a silly joke now.

Too far away to hear me? He's gone — there won't be our day of sitting by a ditch as old men and talking about a fight we took part in one hundred years ago. Maybe it's as well.

I think of old Hector Winslow, eighty-four years of age and dying, running a message on radio and in the newspapers to find his one sister to visit him before he passed on. He hadn't seen her since the First World War when he came west from New Brunswick.

He'd no idea if she'd married, or if she was even alive. Two letters came to him — one from Vancouver and the other from Winnipeg. Both claimed to be his sister, and both excused themselves from visiting him because of the distance. We all felt both letters were frauds, written by small crooks who make a business of writing letters to sick, weary people. But old Hector made out a will right there in hospital, splitting his property two ways and saying it was to be given to the two women who wrote him.

If Jim only knew how we bought a cow at an auction sale, I think he would have laughed and known why we were as we were.

Auctions are still held once a week on the willow flats just the other side of town. My father and I went at least once a month. Most times we didn't bid on anything. But this one time we had money for a cow, so we walked into town, planning to walk the cow home and so save transport costs.

The auction mart was an old, sagging barn with a plank platform out front. The thin, hunched auctioneer used to stand on the platform surrounded by heaps of junk, used furniture, old crockery, leaning clothes pillars loaded with second and third-hand clothing. There was sacks of meal, salt and left-over fertilizer. Much of the stuff was stained and damaged by being left out in the rain all week.

My old man and I pushed our way through the morning crowd of yawning farmers, run-down spectators who didn't have thirty cents to take in the movie in town, and kids who made a million-dollar bid and ran like hell before the auctioneer or his clerk could catch them! A wind blew up in our faces and I pulled down my cap to cut off the smell of wet ammonia fertilizer and rotting upholstered furniture. Nobody said much, and when the auctioneer came on the platform all muttering petered out and there was silence.

The auctioneer fixed up his glasses, cleared his throat and clapped his hands together twice. This was his signal that the auction had begun. Lame Willy, his clerk, immediately led a cow from the barn behind up in front of the platform where we could see it.

"Now what am I bid for this lovely, three-year-old Jersey . . ." the auctioneer fired off, leaning forward as if sniffing the air for how things would go this morning.

"That's no Jersey — that's a Shorthorn!" A big man with a handle-bar moustache hollered at him roughly. There was a tired 'haw-hawing' of laughter from all over, and then silence once more.

"Oh!" The auctioneer took off his glasses and cleaned

them with this thumb, then put them back on his head. He bent over for a closer look at the cow in front and below him.

That's the head you're looking at — ass is on the other end!" snorted the moustache, and there was more 'haw-hawing' than before. The auctioneer acted like he'd come across the surprise of his day.

"Well, goddamn isn't that something! It *is* a Short-horn . . . what do you know! A lovely three-year-old Shorthorn. What do I hear? What am I bid? Come on, gentlemen — what offers do I hear? Don't just think a bid — speak up!"

My old man stabbed his fist into the air and shouted:

"A hundred dollars!"

"A hundred dollars from the man with the check shirt and grey hat!" The auctioneer turned quickly to us then away without slowing his patter.

"A hundred dollars for this lovely, three-year-old Short-horn! Do I hear any offers? Gentlemen — this would be a giveaway! For a hundred dollars I'd buy the cow myself! A hundred dollars is the bid — what do I hear?"

"A hundred and ten!" The bicycle moustache coughed out, his shoulders coming up as if he was squaring for a fight.

"A hundred and ten! I am bid a hundred and ten . . . who'll raise that to a hundred and twenty? She's worth every cent of that and more than a bargain — do I hear a hundred and twenty?" The auctioneer was swinging now. He was on fire, bending to us as if to catch us all in his hands and squeeze all the sense out of us. I saw little beads of sweat break out on his face and run down his neck.

"A hundred and fifteen!" Again my old man.

The auctioneer smiled just a little.

"A hundred and fifteen — the man with the check shirt and grey hat! Gentlemen — quickly now! Let's move this beautiful Shorthorn to meadow — quickly! Who'll give me a hundred and twenty? Do I hear a hundred and twenty? No further bids? Come now — no further bidding? A hundred and fifteen once . . . twice . . . SOLD! To the gentleman in the check shirt and grey hat for a hundred and fifteen dollars!"

The moustache spat a big oyster into the dust, stared hard at my father, and grunting like a wounded boar, walked away.

That wasn't the end of the business, however.

When my old man went up to pay for the cow, he first made a thing of pinching and feeling its legs, prodding its rump with his thumb, kneading under the neck. Then he took the cow's mouth into his hands and opened it. Lame Willy was fidgeting behind with his open ledger, waiting for the money. Even the auctioneer was standing still now, looking down at this inspection with a puzzled frown. I watched my father shake his head slowly and nod for Willy to come over. They had a short talk. Willy seemed scared. He closed his ledger and went over to call the auctioneer himself down.

By now my old man seemed like he was working up into a proper small fury. He started lipping off at the auctioneer while the guy was still coming down off the platform. Then he opened the cow's mouth to show Willie and the auctioneer something. They looked into the cow's mouth, and the auctioneer caught his head in his hands as if trying to hold back a sudden headache. He said something to my father, who made a 'to hell with it' motion with his hand and started walking away. The auctioneer came after him, tapping him on the shoulder. They stopped, talked some more, then shook hands. My father then dug into his pocket, paid Willie, and called me over to take the cow away. The auctioneer was back on the stand now, and the sale continued.

"What was wrong? What happened?" I asked as we led the cow through the willow flats on the way to town. My old man threw his head back and laughed until tears came into his eyes.

"Serves the stupid bastard right," he said, wiping his eyes and fanning his face with his hat.

"What'd you do?"

"I knocked fifteen dollars off the price of this milk sack, that's what I've done!" He started to laugh again.

"We got it for a hundred — is that it?"

"Sure, we got it for a hundred! You remember he didn't know the difference between a Jersey and a Shorthorn?"

"Yeh — but . . ."

"I was counting on him not knowing anything else about stock. So I points out to him he was taking me by selling me a bad cow. A cow that didn't have teeth in its top jaw!"

"You mean to say this cow got no teeth in its top jaw?" I was wondering what mama would say when she found out. My old man grinned.

"No, boy — no cow got teeth in its top jaw! Here — you get behind and drive her faster. We've got to get through town before he finds out an' comes after us . . ."

So you see, while my brother was away learning about music, history, electricity and law — I was here learning how to buy a cow for less.

* * *

The most beautiful girl between here and town is Sophie Makar. She never married, and she won't marry. Hers is the kind of beauty that don't ever marry. It's meant for something else, and here there's nothing else but to marry, farm and raise kids, so she's out.

I knew her as a kid. Even then she'd stand back and watch. Her father, Dan Makar, was a widower and a better farmer than any for miles around. So when she stood back as a kid, I figured at the time it was because she was putting on airs and not wanting to mix with roughs like us.

Then she got older and her great breasts pressed hard against her clothes and her eyes got clear and wild, then we all began to step away from her. Her white skin turned dark with a touch of far-off gypsy; and her hair went uncut until she could wrap it around her long neck. She was wild, strange . . . and so beautiful you got so you'd be afraid to look her in the eye because you knew she could do something to you if she wanted. The women, my mother among them, stepped aside when Sophie approached on the road. It was almost as if she were the queen — the very best among them.

Then dumb Freddy, the idiot, came around.

I was still a kid the summer he came. It was the year we got a good oats crop and everyone took to raising hogs to use up the extra feed the oats made. It was a Sunday afternoon at the general store, and on Sundays when the weather was warm and a nice wind blowing from the south, there were always a few people around the store.

We saw the rug pedlar coming up the road. He pulled up at the store, honking the horn of his car and waving. We stood around watching as he came out of the car. He was a small man, with a Hitler moustache under his nose and whisky pouches under his eyes. His chin was small and came down quickly to his neck from his lips. It wasn't the kind of face you wanted to talk to or do business with. But he came out, carrying a short polished walking stick in his hand.

"And how are all you good people today?" he asked in too-loud a voice, and then he had himself a loud laugh when no one said anything in reply.

"Hey — any of you want to see a monkey?"

He pointed the stick at me and I crossed my eyes to watch the end of it. This really broke him up with laughter. He had to take out a handkerchief and blow his nose before he could speak again.

Now isolated as we are here, a lot of characters have

come around promising to show us things. Some promised to show rain during a dry spell, others said they could bring back a dead mother. This one had his monkey, but nobody was biting. And then Sophie Makar took a step towards the pedlar and stared at him, her eyes wide open and steady as those of a cat.

The pedlar saw her and the smile left his face as he looked around to see if someone was trying a fast one on him. When he saw everyone was half-asleep and not caring if he was here or gone, he unlocked the trunk of his car and took a few pokes inside with his stick.

"Come out!" he called.

I heard a grunt, and then a pair of worn, cracked boots came out on the ends of thin, scarred legs. We all crowded closer now, and watched this man push himself out of the car trunk. He was dressed in tight, patched and repatched jeans and in a shirt from which his elbows came out. His hair looked as if it hadn't been cut from the winter before and a patchy beard sprouted here and there on his face.

His eyes must've hurt in the sun, because he blinked hard and they watered. Then he began to see us standing watching him and the pedlar, and his face broke into the loose grin of an idiot. His eyes were grey, dull and dead.

"Dance for the people, monkey!" the pedlar ordered.

The idiot didn't seem to hear him, and the pedlar swung his stick and hit him across the knees. The idiot staggered under the blow and pressed himself against the car, putting one hand up in front of his face.

"See - you've got yourself a monkey to look at! If you stand close you'd say he looks a bit like a man, even speaks like a man, but he has the brain of a monkey." The pedlar was swinging his stick like a fan in front of his face as he spoke in his loud sing-song voice. He turned to the idiot again.

"All right, monkey, dance for the people. Tra-la-la-la — like this! Dance!"

The pedlar did a quick-step in front of the idiot, who now squinted like he had a pain in his head. One of the farm women among us laughed nervously. The pedlar heard and suddenly got mad. Raising his hand he slapped the idiot so hard the poor devil lost his balance and fell on the dust of the road, where he lay quivering and covering his head with his large, twisted hands.

The pedlar turned to us again and tried to smile, but his eyes were bloodshot with anger.

"Sorry, folks — guess there won't be a show today. To keep a monkey obedient you got to cut back on his food. This one's fed too much. And now if you ladies will come up to the car I'll show you rugs such as you've never seen before! Colours? My, I've got rugs in colours you've never even seen!"

He opened the car door and brought out his sample bag. He had to step over the idiot to get back to us and doing so he kicked the lying man in the ribs. The idiot twisted slowly with pain.

"No . . ." He groaned pitiably. At that moment I was shoved to one side and Dan Makar stepped out of the crowd and reached out to grab the pedlar by the arm.

"Ouch! Lemme go!" The pedlar dropped his samples and tore at Dan's hand. But Dan was a big man with iron wrists and the sad head of Abe Lincoln. The rug man looked up at him and wilted like a little girl.

"Now you git into this car of yours, turn around and beat it just as fast as it can go before you make me more sore than I am right now!" Dan said softly, but his voice had an edge to it I'd never heard before.

"Sure, sure. I've got no argument with you, brother!" The pedlar whimpered and broke away from Dan. "Come on, monkey — back in your cage! People don't like fun here!"

The pedlar picked up his case and stick and stood over the idiot, who lay on the road, but now with his head lifted. He was watching an army of ants creep through the dust in front of his face and he did not hear the pedlar.

"Come on, monkey!" the pedlar repeated, throwing his samples roughly into the car. The idiot was chuckling now and putting his finger in front of the ants, trying to stop them. They moved over his finger and he laughed like a kid.

"Come on!" The pedlar's anger busted out and he came at the idiot with boots and stick.

"Father! Stop him!" Sophie Makar shouted, herself jumping forward and pulling at the pedlar. Then Dan Makar was at her side. With one hand he picked the pedlar a foot off the ground by his shirt front. He swung and threw him against the car. The huckster was scared now, with all the stuffing shaken in him. Picking himself up carefully, he moved around to his door of the car and drove off, forgetting to close the trunk lid, which bobbed up and down like the tail of a galloping horse.

"Now, Dan — what we going to do with *him*?" Pete Wilson, the store-keeper asked, pointing to the idiot. Dan scratched his chin and squatted down beside the fellow.

"No one's going to hurt you now. What's your name?" he asked.

"Freddy," the idiot replied, sitting up.

"Freddy what?"

"Freddy what . . ." the idiot repeated and laughed. Dan got to his feet and turned to the store-keeper. "I'll take him. He'll earn his food and keep at my place. Here — give him a bottle of Orange Crush."

Dan handed Wilson the money for a bottle of pop.

When evening came and Dan walked home with Sophie, Freddy followed ten or fifteen steps behind. My folks and I walked as far behind Freddy, and we were followed by the Bayracks. Once in a while Dan and Sophie would turn and tell Freddy to hurry up and walk with them. He'd smile and run a few steps like they wanted. But his boots hurt his feet, and half-limping he'd slow down, looking around and listening all the time to the sounds of a country evening. Soon he was walking alongside my father. Another mile and he was behind us.

Freddy took his time learning work. But he learned to do simple jobs as good as anyone else. He was passed from farm to farm and there was always work for him cutting wood, cleaning barns or repairing fences. He even learned to milk cows. He took his meals wherever he worked, and slept in empty granaries and in haylofts of barns. People he worked for would chip in money and buy him clothes, and kids were warned not to tease him or throw things at him.

He was stubborn, but farmers found they could break him from sulking by seeming to give in to him when he got sore at something. Even my old man did it once and Freddy melted like butter.

"Doggone it, Freddy, you're right. Don't know what got into me to say you were lining up those fenceposts wrong!"

The next year Freddy started to get wages for his work when people thought he'd learned how to buy his own clothes and tobacco. The wages were nothing much — the odd buck here and there, but Freddy dressed and seemed to have enough left over for chocolates and soft drinks on Sundays.

He became quite a guy for soft drinks. I've seen him open a bottle in Wilson's store, take a long sip from it, closing his eyes and letting the liquid run down the sides of his mouth. Then he'd look around and hoot, "Goot! Goot! You want?"

And he'd offer the bottle to anyone near him.

The second summer Freddy was among us, Sophie Makar got stranger than she'd ever been before. Maybe this was the time she should've married, but like I've told you, Sophie could never marry. Where does one find a man for a woman like her?

Day after day she'd comb her long, heavy hair until it shone with fire in the sun. Then she'd show up one Sunday or on a Saturday in town dressed in the roughest, oldest overalls and man's shirt, her head low and her cheeks dark and angry. She wouldn't speak to anyone. The following day she might come over to borrow a crescent wrench for Dan, and she'd be laughing, her big eyes full of life and fun.

One evening the moon was up and it was too hot to sleep. I heard my folks get up, make themselves a cup of tea and go out into the yard to drink it. I got up and went to sit with them. As we sat there, listening and thinking of nothing, we heard footsteps of someone running. In a moment she was dashing past that gate, her long hair trailing in the breeze, her head thrown back and her white teeth gleaming in the night.

"What's that?" my old man asked in a whisper.

"Come to sleep." My mother gathered the cups and there was a bit of fear in her voice when she spoke. "It's Dan's girl — she walks and runs by herself nights. It's dangerous — something will happen!"

"How do you know?"

"I just feel it will, that's all." My mother shook her head and went in.

One Sunday soon after, Freddy bought a chocolate bar and after biting it himself, offered it to Sophie, who happened to be standing behind him in the store waiting to buy herself an ice-cream cone. Sophie laughed lightly and took the entire bar and ate it. Then to the surprise of everyone she said:

"You're sweet on me, aren't you, Freddy? You like your little Sophie, no? Bet you're dying inside to coddle up to her and give her a squeeze! You're a dear boy, Freddy!"

And just like that she takes Freddy's face in her hands and kisses both his cheeks. The idiot blew the rest of his money on chocolates and gave them all to her.

It was here at our place that Freddy was called in the week after to help butcher our meat for the winter. We only had a hog to butcher, but it's always wise to have an extra hand in case the hog breaks his rope or gets frightened before he's tied down properly. Nothing happened so Freddy just hung around. But during the killing itself, he came up so close we had to get him to move back. When we were bleeding the carcass, he stepped right up to the bucket. Dipping his finger in the warm blood, he licked on it. Then he turned sick, and my old man had to lead him away while mama and I started the dressing down.

The next Sunday, Freddy was at the store again. He bought himself a straw hat, and when Sophie showed up, he stuck close behind her.

"Come on . . . play ball." He invited her, and covered his face as he laughed with pleasure when she stepped outside the store. They played catch-ball most of the afternoon. I was sitting on the steps outside the store. My father and Dan Makar came out and stood above me to share a smoke.

"It's wrong, Dan," my old man said. "It's wrong for Sophie to carry on with the fellow. He's spending all he earns on her. It's asking for trouble."

"Don't I know it," Dan growled. "I could spank her into sense when she was a kid — but now, I can't do anything. You've seen enough to know she'll always get her way. It's my fault. The kid should've had a mother — any mother. Too late now . . ."

Sophie stepped on a sharp stone just then and gave a little cry of pain. She limped away from the game she and Freddy were having and went into the store. Freddy stood outside for a long while, then his lower lip hung down sullenly. He moved past me and the two men above me and followed Sophie into the store. I asked my old man for a nickel and went in myself.

Freddy was standing right behind Sophie, staring at her neck. His face was red with anger and he was breathing quickly, his breath bubbling at the corners of his mouth.

"Come on — play!" He spoke loudly. She moved among the women. He stayed right behind her.

"Come on — play!"

"Go away!" she almost shouted as she turned on him. "What you sniffing at me like that for?"

Then she was heading for the door. He jumped in front of her.

"I buy you chocolate — okay?" He bent his head to her, his lower lip covering his top one with stubbornness.

"No! I don't want your damned chocolate!" Sophie clenched her fists. "Now get out of my way!"

"I buy you chocolate — sure! I buy you pop drink . . . sure! You love me? Okay?" His face crinkled like that of a cornered, hurt dog. "I take you home. Come on."

He reached out and caught her arm. Sophie screamed and tore out of his grasp. She was quivering with rage now, and her eyes were bright and sharp.

"Leave me alone, will you!"

"I walk you home. Come on!" Freddy reached for her again, but she jumped back. Only now she was backed against the counter. I saw Wilson moving to the back door to call for help among the men outside and around the front.

"Go shovel manure or split wood, you crazy fool!" Sophie spat at him. "Go on! You're stupid as a sack of potatoes! You want me to walk with you? I hate the sight of your ugly, stupid face, you know that!"

Freddy bit his lips and blood spurted and trickled down his chin.

"She think — I crazy! She laugh at me! I fix her!" He was a baby kid now, bawling. Dan opened the door behind me. Freddy saw him, ducked and slipped out before Dan was able to figure out what was going on.

"What's the matter here?" he asked. The women looked at him, but none seemed able to explain to him.

Freddy worked and stayed at the Tippets' that week.

When Mrs. Tippet got home that evening, she saw Freddy out in the garden, honing the breadknife on a stone. She asked what he was doing.

"Something," the idiot replied and walked away from her, still sharpening the knife.

The rest happened quickly.

That night, Dan Makar heard his daughter rise and dress in her room, as she had risen and dressed every night for months past. Then she left the house for her nightly run.

And this night when Sophie came down the road near the store where there was a tall border of poplar and alder, Freddy suddenly jumped out from behind a poplar. He stood in front of her, holding a long breadknife belonging to the Tippets.

"Now, Freddy . . . you know I love you and you're a dear boy!" Sophie was scared and started walking backwards. She tried to remember if she'd seen any lights nearby so if she shouted for help there were people up and around to hear her. But she couldn't remember. And Freddy was gaining on her, his arms apart and his movement like those of a wild animal stalking for the kill.

"You . . . not love! You love! You laugh! I do — what I see do to pig!" Then he lunged. Sophie's heel caught in a rut and she fell backwards. She screamed, but her cries were choked in Freddy's sweat-drenched shirt which fell over her mouth. She tried to fight, but the idiot had the strength of another man in his passion. Then she froze as he lowered the razor-sharp blade to her face.

She said she never felt the pain of the blade cut deep into her cheek.

Then Freddy stopped cutting, and with the fingers of his free hand he reached up to touch her injured face. When he felt the blood he had drawn, he lifted his fingers to his lips and licked at them. Then with a terrible cry he sprang to his feet, dropping the knife. She watched him run off the road on to the fields and become lost in the silent night.

He ran, and he ran, and he ran. In the morning they found him where the creek meets the river, in the place I swam every summer. Here Freddy died of a heart burst with exhaustion. The tears were still wet on his swollen face. His fingers, like some twised hooks, hung in the clear water of the creek.

Sophie is still around, more beautiful than ever. More woman, and more strange, distant and fiery. I saw her last Easter — watched her in church. She didn't know I was watching and thinking of all that happened. So I saw her forget herself and absent-mindedly brush a finger along the thin, white scar which runs from just under her eye down her cheek to her throat. It's a strange scar — once you saw it you'd never forget it.

For it gives her beautiful face just a touch of cruelty.

* * *

You ever cup the face of a dog or cat you liked and pressed your own nose against it? The odour of the face or hair is the odour of the love you had for that animal. The same with touch. I'll close my eyes and you put an axe or hammer handle into my hand and I'll tell you if it's been used one, two, three or ten years. Bring it up to your nose and you can smell work in the wood. It's the scent of sweat, tobacco, iron and earth. Maybe those are the things all work is made of.

I've gone through a life touching objects Jim never knew existed. In fact, there are things I've touched my parents never knew, and they lived longer. But because I touched them, they belonged to all of us.

I've stood by the church and run my hand over the red brick of its walls and learned a truth few books tell about. The truth of dedication.

The kind of dedication hunch-backed Joe had when he cycled the countryside at seventy years of age, pleading,

72

arguing, humbling himself like a damned beggar to find labour and money with which to build his church.

"If I die without my church it'll be like I never lived at all. What is land or a house? They can burn or be buried under a dust storm. But a church! It is the house of God, and He will watch over it and protect it!"

Tone-deaf himself, Joe led a band of women carollers up and down the drifted roads each Christmas, singing at every house they could reach. If the farmer didn't give as much as he might, Joe would stop to argue, and threaten to sing more carols by himself if the donation couldn't be bettered!

In summer, when the neighbourhood came out for the few ball-games, there would be hunch-backed Joe canvassing among the people.

It took Joe seventeen years to lift his church from the soil — and you'd have to see it to understand at seven cents a brick how much went into it. We all came out to see it opened for services — all of us, believers or not. It was for Joe's sake we had to go.

Joe was there at the door, his eyes wet with tears he was so proud. He wore a nice black suit and white shirt that must have been his son's because it was too big around the neck. My folks shook his hand and told him it was a good thing to see this day and they knew how happy he was.

The minister came late. We'd all been sitting around for about an hour, although I didn't mind it. I was looking at the coloured glass windows the sun was shining into. Wax candles were lit all over, and I liked their smell. Mother sat with her eyes closed, and my old man was looking and touching the wooden seats and floor — feeling the wood and finish with his fingers and pricing it. He kept turning and fidgeting a lot. When he put his foot on a floorboard under his seat and found it squeaked, he was happy and sat still.

When the minister finally came he turned out to be a

young kid from the city. You could tell from his face, eyes and way of looking at all of us that he'd never missed a square meal in his life, and that he really didn't give a damn for anything in particular. Joe walked beside him to the pulpit, trying to touch his arm. But this kid preacher never even gave the old man as much as a look or a smile.

He gets himself standing in the pulpit, and without so much as explaining why he's late, he gets right down to business:

"Before I begin the opening service, I would first like to collect the certificate of ownership. Is the chairman of the building committee here?"

As he asked this, he took out a pair of glasses and set them on his soft nose. Nobody moved or spoke. Simply because there was no such thing as a building committee. There was only old Joe, riding his bicycle, collecting, singing. He was standing in front of the pulpit now, looking foolish and not knowing what was happening.

"The chairman of the building committee? Or doesn't he go to church?" The kid preacher asks again, a wise little smile on his face now. Joe cleared his throat and spoke.

"What is it you wish, Reverend? Maybe I can help."

The preacher kept smiling as he looked down at the hunched old man.

"Did you build this church yourself, my friend?" he asked, like he was talking to a kind of countryside funny-boy.

"Why — yes! Yes, I did!"

The grin went.

"Oh, I see . . . I must explain that if I'm to preach here as minister of our faith, I will require ownership of the church to be turned over to the area council. Otherwise, anybody could just walk in and preach a service!"

"I wouldn't let them!" Joe stuck his chin out like he meant it. The preacher began to pick up his satchel and move down from the pulpit.

74

"In that case I'm afraid there will be no opening service today!"

There was a bit of a growl among the people in the church, which Joe mistook as anger against him.

"Wait! Wait!" he called out. "Whatever you want — if I got to sign something . . ."

There was a paper to sign all right. They used the pulpit to sign it on. When it was over with, the preacher started to look holy, but Joe was beaten. He walked out with his head down and his hands gripping the bottom of his suit coat. When the service was over, we found the old man standing by the church gate, crying like his heart was breaking apart. The preacher walked past and drove away in his nice new Chevrolet car like Joe never existed. But we all stopped to hear him when he raised his head and saw us.

"As God is my witness, I renounce this church and what faith I had that made me build it! I'd sooner pray in the bush than enter a place where — where business is made on the pulpit!" He brought each word up like it was wrapped in barbed wire, tearing his throat to shreds. Then he walked away from the churchyard. All the neighbours started talking out the rights and wrongs of what happened, but Joe's wife and family were having none of this foolishness.

"It's our business — so stop it!" His wife had a high voice that cut you wherever you stood. She had her hair curled in town for this day, and seeing her I could tell how worked up she'd gotten over Joe's humiliation. At home she must've had three or four fried chickens to feed the new preacher, and new curtains on the windows and cloth on the table. Now the preacher was gone, and she somehow felt Joe was to blame for it all.

"Joe! Don't disgrace us!" she called after him. He didn't turn, so she went after him, her sons and daughters trailing in a long line behind her.

When we drove past their gate on our way home, Joe was sitting on the porch, holding his head in his hands. She was giving him her tongue. He waved for her to go away.

"I have said what I had to say, now leave me be!" he pleaded.

"Such shame you have brought down on us! Ask those people to stop and eat with us!" She pointed to us. "Our children have to live here — and I have to blush for you. Say to somebody you didn't mean what you said and you'll do what the preacher asks!"

With all his nice clothes on, Joe went to bed. He lay in bed two days without rising or asking for food. On the third day he died of a broken heart.

At Easter of that year they raffled off his bicycle to help buy a bell for the church tower.

* * *

I like mushrooms. In all the years I have lived here I must've gathered and eaten a ton of mushrooms. Times are changing. They say mushroom picking now is taking too much time for what one gets out of it. I continue to pick, even when others no longer do so. There is really no one who picks in this neighbourhood, and the last two years I have had full run on all mushrooms in a two-mile area around this house. I have my favourite spots, like the other side of the meadow, where you'll find plenty an hour or two after a light shower. When these heavy rains pass, there'll be at least four places they'll be coming up thick as buttons. If you stay until tomorrow, I'll take you along.

To reach one of the mushroom patches, I follow an old cowpath that goes across what was once a pasture for everybody's cattle. A few years ago, some cows got hoof and mouth disease and the cattle were taken away and pastured at home to keep it from spreading. I like this meadow, although since they stopped grazing it, there's a new crop of young alders coming up. The meadow was once an old and dry stream bed. It's not far from here, and a nice walk when you feel like a walk.

I'm not a good or heavy thinker. But I can think a lot when I'm alone searching for mushrooms. I even talk to myself knowing there's no one to hear me. Can you tell me why talking to yourself is wrong? Have you never done it? I've talked to stones I rolled and trees I cut. I've talked to our cattle and horses. Farmers, lonely men, talk to themselves — they have to.

If you knew her you'd say Marta Walker would never talk to herself. She's married to Eric Walker, and that's their house over there — first neighbours to the south of here. Marta was a teacher at our school for a few years before she married Eric. He's quite a bit older than she and had worked too hard to take time to marry — but that's before she came here.

I don't know how they met, but soon they were going around a bit, and when she finished teaching she went over to his house. My old man said when he saw her once she'd said she was housekeeping for Eric for the summer months. Then we heard they'd married. When school opened in the fall, she didn't apply to go back to teaching.

I've told you that Eric was older, but Marta looked older than she really was. She'd come from an unemployed coal-mining family in Drumheller. Some kind of operation when she was a young girl made her hair grey. A lot of hard times at home and getting through school made her face tight and serious. She would look you in the eye and act like she saw right through you. Yet one day I saw her in town walking along with Eric, and I was in for quite a surprise.

She'd let her hair down and had used some lipstick on her mouth — and damned if that didn't make her look a

grey-haired eighteen! Nice, too. Eric looked like he was
her father, and he seemed to know it, because she nodded
to me a "hello" but he didn't even look my way. Now if
you want to see a sour face any day of the week, you need
only look at Eric Walker.

"He smiled once only," my old man used to say. "And
that was the time Swift's made a mistake and paid him for
three steers when he'd only shipped one to them. But they
found out and he had to give the money back, and he's
never smiled since!"

The story may be true, it may not. But I saw another
story much later which told me everything about them, and
a lot about myself. I was picking mushrooms and thinking
a lot because I'd been working hard and was put off with
how little money I was making and getting more and more
tired because my stomach wasn't right. I was getting pains
that brought me to my knees in a sweat.

"It's something you ate," my old man reckoned.

My mother figured it was growing pains. I kept on
working, but the pain wasn't getting better. So I had a lot
to think about. Which is why I walked right on Marta
without hearing or seeing her first. She was sitting under
an alder just off the cowpath, holding her face in her hands
and moaning to herself. Her hair hadn't been combed and
was hanging down over her face and fingers.

"Mother of God!" she was saying in a pleading, sad
voice. "What have I done? No childhood . . . no happiness
ever, and now I have this. Four pots to wash every day —
two beds to make. And then I should find him some place
in the fields . . . a man? Eric! Eric! A stuffed sack would
be no different! Not a word since Thursday morning.
If he isn't working, he is eating or sleeping. Why did I
marry? Why?"

I stood over her, wanting to run for my face burned
with shame at finding her — so undressed. I couldn't
move. I knew if I moved she would see me right off and

I could never run from her, and her knowing that I heard all. What was there to do? I got down on my knees in front of her and gave her my handkerchief.

"It ain't clean," I told her. "But it's good for a wipe yet."

She was on her feet like a deer that's been shot at and missed. Her face turned white, and her eyes became big and scared.

"You've been standing — listening to me?" she asked in a whisper. I nodded. The colour was coming back to her cheeks now and her eyes were mad.

"What business you got listening? Do you look into windows when people sleep? Is that the kind of boy you are?"

"I didn't hear what you said!" I lied, and she knew I lied. She laughed.

"I didn't really," I kept on. I sounded foolish listening to myself speak, and I was getting hot and prickly all over. She laughed again and then *I* got sore.

"So what's funny?" I almost shouted at her. "You think I want to hear all this crap about you and your old man? I been walking this path before you even came here, so it's not my fault! Anyway, what I heard don't matter. I won't say nothing to nobody."

"I know you wouldn't, or I'll put you in jail!" She was going to throw everything in my face now — I could see it in her eyes and her face — angry, hurt and a little bit frightened. "You want to see something?"

Right then she reaches up to her throat and grabs the collar of her dress. With one pull she tears it open down to her stomach, showing me one of her naked breasts. Then she seems scared of what she did and pulls the dress together with both hands.

"If you say anything, I'll tell you did that to me! If not, I'll say it caught on a branch and tore!" She turned away and looked as if she was going to cry or run screaming from me. But now I was scared. I ran before she did. When I got back to this yard, I couldn't come in because I was on fire. So I pulled up a bucket of icy water from the well and splashed it over my head until my eyes hurt with the cold.

* * *

Yes, the last few years I've been working this farm, but there's nothing in it for me. Between the bank, grocery store and this religious hostel that's been milking me ever since my mama went to work for them, I don't get enough left to buy myself shoelaces when the crop's sold! If I get the debts cleared, if I live that long — then it might be different.

I still do some stone-picking, like I did for years before. I used to move from farm to farm as new land was broken, and I'd lift the stones and boulders from freshly-turned soil and haul them off the fields. Here behind my belt I carried a small hatchet to cut out long roots that the plough hadn't turned. You'd have to get as many roots out as you could find, or they'd tangle in other machinery when the farmer tried to work the new fields down for seeding.

I once read a book on American prisoners working on chain gangs busting rocks for roads. Compared to stone-picking here, a chain-gang was a holiday. There's no hotter, harder or dirtier work going. It stoops your back and turns your hands into claws which take years to straighten out again. And you're lucky if that's all the damage you got off with. I've known guys with hernias operated on so many times there was hardly anything left to stitch together any more.

Why did I work like this? Same reason I still do a spell of stone-picking — it's about the only job around that pays money for wages and lasts more than a day or two. Oh, there's some work on road repairs but you've got to have pull for those jobs, like you got to be a bit of a hammer-boy for the Social Credit party, because we're still an improvement district and everything we get here we get because the party wants it that way. When I see a farmer riding a road maintainer, I know how he voted last time in the provincial elections, or how he sold his vote and the votes of all his family for the next election. Even though he swears on a stack of Bibles it's not so.

Hey — you ever meet anyone who *admits* he votes Social Credit? I've never. It's like a disease they won't talk about. Yet they got forty-six votes here two years back. So we've got forty-six liars living here, or somebody's mighty handy with opening and closing ballot-boxes between the time of voting and the time the ballots are counted.

We work as stone-pickers for money. Big money. Four dollars a day with grub thrown in. Sometimes, even a place to sleep.

We work alone. We work in pairs. For a while I worked by myself, because I was still a kid and scared and needing to find my own feet. But about the time of the business with Marta Walker, I began working with a partner. His name was Hank. He was a German and he stood over six feet tall and weighed two hundred and fifty pounds. He was a heavy work machine, lifting and carrying away boulders I couldn't even roll.

"You take little vons, I take the big!"

We worked like that, and pretty soon we were on piece-work and making six dollars a day each. But we couldn't work through the summer together. We quarrelled over women.

Hank had ugly things to say about women. I listened, and one day told him about the afternoon I found Marta Walker. He got a big laugh out of that.

81

"If it vas me, boy, I'd of give her a couple in the mouth! She'd stay home then!"

"She didn't know I was there."

"If voman takes dress off in front of me like dat, I kill her!"

"Why?" Again I was choking and my face burned.

"Vot's the matter, kid? You tink woman is like man? You tink?" He growled like a dog.

"They hurt like men, Hank. They're no different!"

"Voman is noting! Noting at all!" Hank snarled and his eyes got mean and small. "Voman is veak, small. Cry like baby. Take dress off. Man don't cry! Man is everytink because he don't cry! Man is like mountain — can take vind, snow, rain! Never change! Alvays the same — alvays strong!"

"Do you hate women?"

"Dat's right — I hate the sonofabitch! Dey try veaken me — ruin me . . . take avay my man-juice an' den my teeth an' hair! Never! I kill her first. Voman never do dat to me!"

I was afraid of him now because he wasn't talking to me. He was shouting at the wind — as if arguing back something he'd done or was going to do. For a moment I was scared for Marta, thinking that he knew her and was going on like this because of what I said about her. Then he stood over me like a giant.

"I hate voman!"

He picked up a two-hundred pound chunk of granite and with a grunt threw it ten feet in the air, his muscles snapping like snakes up his arms and down his legs. The rock hit the earth with a whomp and drove itself completely into the ploughed ground. Hank bared his teeth and laughed a wild stallion whinny. I never went back to stone-picking with him. He was fair enough to leave my half of the money with the farmer we'd worked for, and the guy brought it to me after Hank quit and went on.

82

I worked alone for a couple of weeks after breaking off with Hank. And then this shrivelled little sonofagun Walt showed up. I was clearing a field and suddenly he was there working with me and I didn't have the heart to say move on for I was here first.

Walt was a terrible man for cursing. Either he never learned to speak properly, or proper speaking couldn't get across what he meant. For he cursed when he was happy, he cursed when he was hungry, and he cursed when he was down and sad. He'd been out to sea. He'd worked on grape and cotton picking in New Mexico and California. He'd followed the tobacco harvest route for many years.

"But my damned luck broke and I end up on stones. This damned dyin' — a little every damned minute. But what the hell — everything's dyin' in this country." He looked up straight into the sun and spat.

"We're making a living, Walt," I said.

"Living? Kid — you don't live here. It's a damned grave-yard, that's what it is. The place of the blasted and dead back in the pines! Will you look at the bloody country? Grey, an' thirsty and hot. Same's the farmers I've seen here. Damn, but I wouldn't stay here if I was paid a million dollars!" He spat again and his skinny face twitched he was that cheesed off.

I pulled off my cap and mopped the muddy sweat on my forehead.

"I've had my fun here."

"Fun?" He looked at me as if I'd lost my bolts. "I've been here since June and I haven't seen or heard anyone laugh, that's how much fun you all have! Hell — whole damned place is for the birds. As soon's I clean this field and the other one I promised, I'm gone — gone for good!"

I came home to sleep at nights, unless I worked more than four miles away. I told Walt to come home with me and we'd throw up a cot for him. But he always went his way at sundown. He didn't even turn into the empty granary that stood on the edge of the field. He brought his grub with him each day — a can of cold beans which he poured over a few slices of bread, washing the mess down with coffee he had asked the boss to bring down in a jar each morning.

But at night he'd throw this old banket roll that came with him everywhere over his shoulder and march away to his sleeping place. I soon learned this was a strawstack of the most vicious barley anyone had grown in these parts for years. Walt showed up for work in the morning with clothes and hair bristling with glass-like barley spikes.

"What you sleeping in a barley stack for, Walt?" I wanted to know. "Those spikes will dig your eyes out."

"I don't mind the spikes. When I sleep, I damned well want to be left alone, an' when I sleep in a barley stack, I'm left alone!" He took his shirt off and picked it clean. I was watching, and wondering how any shirt could pick up and hold so much dirt, for it was shiny black.

"You being bothered in your sleep, Walt?"

"Not now. But other times I've been."

"What do folks want to bother a man for?"

"Not damned folks — it's the cows come nosing around that gives me the bloody willies! You ever been waked by a cow licking your face? It's like a wet rasp file!"

"I never been licked by a cow. Once by a calf, but never a cow. Funny a cow should want to lick you. I never had that happen to me."

"It's the damned salt they're after, boy. They can smell the salt before they see you," he said, looking wise and old.

"Why don't you wash, Walt? It'd take the salt off you."

"Aw, for the love of Christ! Talk to a kid . . ." He spat a fast zipper through his teeth and, putting his shirt on, went back to work. I liked him, dirty clothes and all. He was what a lifetime of living on road-dust had made him, and it wasn't all bad, the way I saw it. We build roads, canals, tall buildings and airfields, as well as pulling in every harvest going. And in the end we wear a shirt and pants to death on ourselves for there is neither the place nor the time to wash and change any more. I'm afraid of filth, for I know when I find it I shall be at first walking and then running downhill. Filth finds us — sometimes on the kitchen floor or the pillowcase, at other times in back of the heart. It is not pain, but in pain one has time to see the filth he has let gather. I've already seen the filth I've gathered, and some of it's worse than Walt's.

I walked with Walt as far as the road when he left. Watched him limp away, going as empty-handed as when he came, with the blanket roll and lunch bag over his shoulder. Going south for the warmer autumn and some tobacco fields he'll find there, and after that the next year and the next on cotton.

Sometimes I bartered my work when money for wages was hard to come by. People barter their hours of labour when there's need to help and be helped, but payment in cash is not possible. Even when the harvest is in and sold, there are taxes and bank loans to settle, clothes to buy for winter. I've had to ask men to help me — yet how do I pay? Last year I come out with thirty dollars to the good — the year's farming, and I got thirty dollars left! You still want to know how our half of the world lives? Smells in our houses will tell you — soap, fried grub and cheap wallpaper.

I bartered my work years ago, even when I was no more than a kid. We all had to. I used to work on harvesting crews, or cutting wood, or putting up fences. I've even dug potatoes. My old man kept count how many days I worked here and there, and when the time came to settle, we'd get a quarter of beef as payment from one neighbour, two days use of a tractor from someone else, and a couple loads of hay when we went short ourselves.

When I was just about full-grown, but not yet a man, Sam Topilko pulled off a stunt which was part of barter living. Sam had a face blue as a piece of suit-cloth. Some liver disease did that to him. He always liked a good argument, particularly if he felt it might save him money or work.

"Now look here," he says to my father. "The kid put in three days stooking oats for me. Now I'll work it back helping to grind hog feed for you — but not three days, no sireee! I'll work back *one* day, and I think that's fair and square!"

He stuck out his chin like he was planning to make a fast fight of it. My old man is no slouch at this game himself. He rammed his hands into his pants pockets and stuck out *his* chin at Sam.

"What in hell you talking about, Topilko?"

Sam stepped back a little. "I'm saying me working a day evens up the three your kid worked for me. That's what I'm saying!"

"Like hell it does, is what *I'm* saying! I got three days coming from you and three days work I'm going to get!" My old man was loud, wide-mouthed, knowing he was going to get his way, and making all the noise he could in the meantime.

Sam Topilko began scratching at his crotch.

"He's only a kid. He can't put in the work a man can. Not that I've any complaints about him, but he's a kid."

My father had Sam, and he was playing with him the way a cat plays a mouse. He narrowed his eyes and snorted at Sam: "Come on now — what in hell you talking about? That kid is stronger than I am. Hey — son!"

I looked up.

"Show this fat prick how you throw a grain-bag full of wheat over your shoulder. Come on — show him!"

Our wagon was standing in the yard, fully loaded with grain to grind. I went over and lifted a sack of wheat down.

"Now lift it as high as you can and put it back on the

wagon," my old man ordered. I took it up over my head, turned twice with it, then heaved it back on the load.

"See that? Did you see that, eh?" he gloated, wagging his finger in front of Sam's blue face. "You had a good look. That kid's made of muscle and bone!"

Sam bit his lip and looked at our wagon. Then we began work. He put in three days for the time he owed us, and never said another word about my worth. I was worth as much as the next man.

Dealing with men, it worked out this way: a man working with a team of horses, as at haying or threshing time, was worth the work of two men. So when I took our team and hayrick, each day I worked out made up two days of some neighbour having to do hand labour in return.

I was getting bigger and stronger every day. Then one day I had to use my strength to hurt. But only once, because word got around and I didn't have to do it again. Yet I was scared sick when it happened.

My old man had taken the team to another farm, leaving me to field-pitch on the farm of Sidney Danzer. Sidney was a nervous, tightened-up sort of guy who went hairy when things weren't going his way. The year I was helping him harvest, they sure weren't going his way at all. The crop was poor, and the machine threshing for him was putting a lot of grain into the straw. He wasn't sleeping good, and on the third day of threshing, he was getting dark rings under his eyes and a guy was taking his life in his hands even talking to Sidney any more.

So I was field pitching for him. The day started hot and dry. By ten o'clock in the morning, the sun was a grey fire dancing up and down with heat waves. The men coming and going were edgy, silent, hot. Soon they drank the water-jug dry and kept going to it even when they knew it was empty. But it gave them a chance to walk away from work and have a bit of a swear to ease up on. The threshing machine was laying down a cloud of brown dust, and soon it would spread and we'd have to breathe it instead of air in the field.

"Li'l bit too hot to work today, no?" said the Indian teamster I was helping to load up. I said it sure was. Then the commotion started near the threshing machine.

We stopped loading and looked over to see Sidney's team bolt, and him hanging on hard and being thrown from one side of the rick to the other as the wagon bounced and whipped over the rough field. Then he got hold of the reins and began lashing the horses into a controlled runaway. I'd seen this done before — giving the runaway team the head until they tired out. But Sidney was wild and was walloping the daylights out of his team.

"If wagon-pole break, they kill him for sure!" the Indian said with a bit of fear in his voice. His team started to snort nervously, and putting down his pitchfork he went to them and held their bridles. Meanwhile, Sidney was keeping his team galloping in a wide circle which he began tightening in to where we were. The team took at least a dozen turns before he brought them up to us and pulled them to a stop. The two dark mares were lathered in their own sweat. I went over to help him load up first so he'd have more time to rest his team before taking the load in.

"What do you want? Get the hell out!" he hollered at me, his hands shaking like he was about to throw a fit. "Get out or I'll put a fork through you! I don't need your bastard help!"

He jumped off the wagon and began loading two and three sheaves at a gime, grunting like it was busting his back. I sort of stood around wondering if I should go back to the Indian, or give Sidney a minute to cool off and help him first. Then I saw a pool of blood gathering under the hoof of the horse nearest me. I went over and saw that she'd jumped the trace, which had torn a deep cut into the inside of her leg. I started to talk to her and slowly undid the trace, bringing it around the outside and fastening it again.

"What you doing?" I looked up to see Sidney standing over me, his eyes red and squinted. The Indian was still standing by his team, staring at us as if we weren't there at all.

"Your horse is hurt." I pointed at the blood.

"It's her or me today! She'll go like that until she drops, and that won't be no loss. Put the trace back where it was!" he ordered.

"No," I said and didn't move. I watched his hands tighten on the handle of his fork.

"You heard me!"

I couldn't and wouldn't move. I tried to swallow the sickness rising up from my stomach and choking my throat.

"You little bastard! I'll put her down with you — if that's what you want! I'm an old man — got piles so bad I can't walk! But don't fool yourself! I'm not too old or weak to bring ya to your knees — I'll teach you I can!"

He stepped back and lifted his fork to stab at me. The acid in my throat was now burning the back of my nose. I took my handkerchief from my pocket and wrapped it around my right fist, for my knuckles were swollen big and painful with work. My knees felt like they'd give. I tried to speak, but the sick fear was on my tongue now, gagging me.

I watched him run at me, the fork held high. He came fast, but I saw every step he took — the hate flowering in his eyes — the pitchfork coming at my head. I saw him bare his teeth for the feel of the steel tines going into my skull. And just before this happened, I came alive — one hundred percent alive! I jumped at him and hit him with all my strength to the side of his cheek. I could feel his jawbone break and saw him fall away, spinning round and round and round. And then he fell beside his wagon and lay still. I turned away and vomited long and painfully.

"You sure hit 'im hard! Betcha he never been hit like dat before!" The Indian was in front of me now, grinning with excitement. I wiped the sour phlegm from my lips with my sleeve.

Then I took my pitchfork and ran all the way home.

* * *

I've been telling you before about this pain I was having in my stomach. It was nothing at first, just a pain that felt like I'd eaten too much of the wrong kind of grub. But pretty soon it was bothering my work, and towards the end it hurt so I had to bite my lips and I was seeing floating specks before my eyes.

"It's just growing pains," my mother kept saying, but I saw her getting worried. Then one day my old man and I went into town to see the doctor. I had to go into hospital a week later and they made an operation to take out a stomach ulcer. When I came around, I saw a nurse standing by my bed. I thought she was laughing, but it must've been the gas playing hell with my ears and eyes, because when I asked her what was funny, I saw her face clear and she wasn't laughing or even smiling.

"What's your name?" I asked, not really wanting to know because I was that weak. I felt I had to keep talking to fight back the weakness and sleep that sat like a black cat under the window.

"Nancy Burla."

"So you're my nurse. You going to make me strong again?"

"I'll try." She came around with a tray from which she gave me some white pills and a glass of water. I took them and went to sleep. During the night I kept waking, burning with thirst. I thought she was by my bed sometimes. At other times I knew how alone I was. I thought I was going to die, not from pain but from a feeling of death and loneliness that I felt would get the best of me before morning.

And then ... and then it was morning again! Outside the hospital window a spruce branch rocked in the wind and blue clouds moved across the sky. I was alive, and outside the building neither the tree nor the milk truck I heard squealing to a stop knew how close to death I had been. This is the scare of death — knowing that your going isn't going to make it rain that day or change a highway you might have helped to build. A few friends around you might know a little of the truth you had to live with one night, many weeks — or that half-second you come up for air and know it is too late — you shall never make it. A little of that truth of your death and nothing else. It's the way it should be. The dead should have no grip on the living. Never, never!

I once watched a neighbour build a tomb for himself in our cemetery. He built it of cement, reinforced with four-inch steel. The damned thing is good for a thousand years. Inside he made a dozen shelves for a dozen coffins to rest in. The coffins were to be left open, so that as more of the family were placed inside, someone would have a chance to see the faces of the ones gone earlier. He and his wife lie in this tomb now. A thousand years — someone will find them, blackened and dried like rotten leather — or prunes.

What is the meaning of this sick sin? Is a man who builds a tomb for himself any better than a guy caught doing something dirty in public? You tell me — you look like you had a half-assed education! Or don't you know nothing about things that hurt, frighten or mix us up?

I'm asking you, you bum!

I've got a right to know what it is you've learned in your schools that I cannot find here to answer my questions!

Jim never talked but in one letter, and then he was only a sad kid, and what he had to say wasn't important to me, because I'd already lived through that kind of doubt and it would never make me think of taking my life.

Tell me something from yourself. You can't just be educated to make new machines that take work away from me without telling me what you are doing and how you are going to help me live! Tell me! You've got ears and mouth the same size I got, yet I'm doing the talking and you the listening! Or, don't you know either? Or are you going to give us a pension and a small hut to sit in, like we've been giving our old ones and the crippled. You're not going to, you know, because I'm going to fight you as I'd of fought Jim. You won't take the world away from me that easy! You haven't proven to me you deserve it.

Ah — don't worry — it's not you I'm shouting at.

Let's see where was I — yes, Nancy Burla was there when I came back to life. And as I sucked up more and more life into me, she seemed to be there giving it out! The clean white uniform, the fast, powerful walk — her way of coping with every problem quickly and gently — she was a world apart from the farm that was killing me. She was life! That is why I felt rotten and mad when my folks came to see me. I didn't talk — wouldn't even look at them.

When I coughed, the stitched wound in my belly hurt so I had to feel down to make sure it hadn't torn open. I couldn't hold back the tears from coming with the pain. They saw this and said nothing.

"We'll be killing a hog for when you come back home, so you get fattened up," my old man said. As he got up to leave he warned me, "Don't let them feed you any peanuts here. Peanuts can kill you after an operation."

"What have peanuts to do with how I am?" I asked. He only shrugged, like he didn't know why, but only that one mustn't. That's another thing about our people — our heads are full of things we mustn't do. We mustn't steal;

we mustn't tell lies; we mustn't want what we can't afford; we mustn't tell anyone how poor we are.

I'm going to ask you something — how many people are there in Canada in the same boat as me? Living on a farm off which they'll never make a thousand dollars a year? And how big are their families that have to be raised on so little? You don't know, because the poorer a man gets the less he wants to talk about how little he's got.

You'll find out if you wanted to stick around for a few weeks. Watch and see what a man with a family eats — how old his furniture and dishes are — how many blankets per bed does he have. Or watch the mortgage men at work, if you've the stomach for that sort of thing. I still chew my lip until I taste blood every time I see the mortgage man come out to a farm where an old man's died.

He's there to sell the place, pay himself and the tax office off, then throw what's left for the family to fight over. Land has to sell at so much per acre. Then there's stock and unsold grain. The furniture and household goods will sell for very little. It all totals up to around four or five thousand dollars. Which sounds like a lot of money, even when half of it goes to paying taxes and loans at the bank. But remember that a man worked thirty-two years of his life to set aside that much, and that he had nothing at all besides this to carry him through sickness, or when he gets too old to work. To get any money at all towards the end of his life, he had to stand back and see his home, farm and family torn apart just to have a few measly dollars come to him.

It makes people cheesed off until sometimes they let go of the rope for a few hours and do the craziest things imaginable. I've seen two men — a white and an Indian — both so drunk they were blind. Each loaded up a .22-calibre rifle and went staggering out into a field of clover. There they started to play war, shooting at each other and ducking down from the shots being returned. The clover field was on a corner of this farm. I climbed into the barnloft and watched. I was afraid they'd kill each other and too afraid to go out and try to stop them. There was always the chance the white man would think me the Indian or the other way around, and both open fire at me and not miss. They shot it out until they reached the end of the supply of shells. Then the white man rolled over and went to sleep. The Indian went stalking through the clover for a while, trying to find him, and then he too lay down and slept. I ran out then and collected both their guns and hid them in the cellar under this house. I'll bet neither of them today remember what they did that day when they both got too cheesed off with living.

At the hospital — when I came to leaving, I had the most awful time. First, they wanted money which I didn't have — to pay for the operation. The doctor seemed more concerned about this than checking out the dressing on my belly. In fact, he never did look at it that day. And I was sort of weak, and worried that nobody had come out to get me. But it was in the middle of haying, a hot, clear day — and the folks just couldn't afford the time to come into town. I'd have to walk home, and I didn't feel up to it. Then this damned doctor was wearing me down.

"How soon can you make a payment on your bill?" he asked, looking at me over his glasses,

"Next time I get into town I'll bring some money."

"How much will that be?"

Nancy Burla came into the doorway. I could smell and feel her all over the room. She didn't speak.

"Have you no idea how much you will pay?"

He made me mad. He had no right rubbing me down in front of the girl. My family and I had done without, but we always paid our way. Any other time wouldn't have mattered so much, but not in front of that girl.

There was a sun-room at the end of the ward, and at

night I went there to sit in the dark and listen to the wind in the spruces outside. Most of the nights were cloudy, and once the wind was so strong it carried dust that chinked against the windows. I used to dream all sorts of crazy dreams in that room. Once I imagined I was a shoe with no lace, and I walked around unbuttoned and coming apart like Hattie Winslow, when her girdle didn't dry in time for the Hallowe'en dance — her clothes just weren't big enough to hold her together!

"A few feet of binder twine would do the job — through the crotch and over both shoulders!" I heard my old man saying to one of the neighbours, but when he saw me he acted like he hadn't said it at all.

So I sat there thinking I was a shoe, and Nancy Burla came in, bringing me a bottle of soft drink.

"How did you know I was here?" I asked.

"Don't have to have high school to know where anybody is in this hospital." She laughed when she said that, and I laughed with her because it really sounded funny.

When we'd laughed ourselves out, we didn't say anything for a long while. We drank our soft drinks. I heard her get up from her chair to go. I could smell her skin with the movement of her clothes, and I felt both angry and happy — wild and tired — all at the same time.

"Pay you back tomorrow," I said. "Haven't got any change with me now."

"That's all right."

I watched her in the lit ward. Her hair bounced as she walked, and she clicked the two empty bottles against each other as she carried them. Before turning the corner down the hall, she threw back her shoulders, half-turned and waved to me. Her body pushed hard against the blouse of her uniform when she did that, and when I went back to bed I couldn't hold back the dream which exploded out of me that night.

"You've got no right saying that!" I said to the doctor, holding my breath back as I spoke so as not to sound too angry.

"Well now, I don't think you're in any position to argue with me, young man. We expect prompt payment, just as you expect prompt treatment when you come to us!" He had this oily, smart-aleck smile on his face now, knowing he was digging where it hurt the most. Some people are like that — they just have to ride somebody to feel complete themselves. I've got a thick callus on the palm of my hand, and when I slammed the table between us a bottle of ink rolled off and broke on the floor, but I didn't feel my hand hurt at all.

"You shut your pig-mouth or I'm going to shut it for you good!" I heard myself holler. The doctor didn't even move his eyes from me. I left him sitting there like he was made of wood.

I paid him off as soon as I could but I didn't go back to have my dressing changed. I did it myself here in this kitchen over a basin of salt water. Yet the next time I was in town, I walked to the hospital soon's I got away from the folks. I didn't see the doctor's car, so I hung around in front, hoping to see Nancy again. She didn't show up that time, but the next trip into town I was in front of the hospital again, and saw her. She was dressed in her ordinary clothes when she came out of the place. Without the white on she looked smaller, more shy. She saw me and came over to where I stood under the spruce tree. She smiled, and then we walked up the hill overlooking the town. We reached a ledge of rock and she said she wanted to sit a while.

"How's your stomach?" she asked.

"All right." I pitched a small pebble playfully at her ankle. She quickly pulled it back under her skirt. But she didn't smile.

"What's eating you?"

"My father's drinking again," she said quietly. She never told me of her father before.

"That's bad, eh?"

"Yes, it's bad. Two years ago he took a pledge. He'll lose the farm if he doesn't stop now, mama says." Then she started to cry. I leaned over to touch her, because I felt so damned sorry for her that I had to show it some way. But when I put my hand on her shoulder, she moved away and got to her feet. She seemed afraid.

"I'm sorry — you mustn't cry. You're so beautiful, Nancy!" I wasn't making any more sense than her tears. I was just that close to tears myself. She only got more scared and started walking downhill in a hurry. I came after her, saying again how sorry I was.

"Leave me alone!" she said in a crying voice. Then she began to run. I stayed alone behind, looking after her until the path turned on the way to the hospital. Then I looked at the town, hot and dusty, with a sign made of white stones imbedded in the hill across the river saying to watch and not start forest fires.

Behind me on this hill was a small farm. I heard a woman holler from the barnyard. A dog barked and a hog squealed long and loud, as if the dog was tearing off its ear with his teeth. Then there was no sound, and I walked down the hill back to town.

* * *

Before you return, we will be sure to visit Sergei Pushkin. Every year there was a big party at his house. It happened just before harvest time, when the hay was in and the barley was a bleached mat on the fields, ready for cutting. Sergei would appear at the gate and shout, "Come to my place tomorrow! We have something to drink and little bit to eat!"

He is a white-Russian émigré, who came to Canada

about the time of the Russian Revolution. He likes his food and he likes his drink. On Saturday nights you can still hear him coming down the road from town, beered-up to the eyes, hollering at his team and the wagon creaking and rattling as he drives along.

"Amerika all right! Gidyap straight ahead, sonsofabitches together!"

If you were to meet him in town or at church and he was thinking about life, he would say:

"Boy, if we was rich, we could go to British Columbia and grow apples! But we are poor, so we stay in the muskeg an' grow weeds and taxes. But that's all right — never have crop failure that way, what you say, boy?"

The day of the yearly party at Sergei's place was in honour of some Russian saint whose name I never learned. It was a special day in Sergei's life, and he once sold a cow to pay for the food and whisky to make a good party for everyone.

It would be sundown by the time we reached his house, and he would stand outside the door with his wife by his side. He'd shake everybody's hand and say, "Welcome to my place, my good friends! Have a good time, please!"

Inside, the main room would already be half-full of his children and grandchildren, who'd also rise and welcome you in. It was ten times more polite than any church party I've gone to, and these people meant every bit of it too.

Always there were candles on the table, surrounded by enough grub to feed an army. Roast beef and pork, sweetbreads, pickles, headcheese, dumplings and holopchi. As we made our way to our seats, his children and grandchildren would wait until we'd all settled down before moving up and taking their places. But before they sat down, they'd wait for Sergei and his wife to seat themselves first.

Like I say, there were candles on the table. They lit up the proud smile Sergei had on his face. Then he'd reach for the whisky bottle in front of him, rise and go around the table, filling all the glasses to the brim. Ending up back at his chair, he'd fill his own glass last and raise it.

"For this year an' next year — and next year after that, an' maybe lots more years if we lucky — good luck and everything be all right for everybody!" he'd propose a toast.

We'd all drink, every man and woman and child over ten. Then we would begin to eat, cold food first to put out the whisky fire in our throats. Everybody was talking now — some laughing, some teasing, and all agreeing about the heat of the whisky and the good taste of the food.

Sergei didn't eat much, for he talked a lot — to us and to his children and grandchildren. In between his talking he drank from the bottle in front of him. Sometimes he broke from his halting English into phrases of Russian. And he drank and asked us all to drink with him. Then he laughed, and after he laughed he wept a little and put his arms around people nearest to him.

"We work like dogs — sometimes go hungry, but I tell you, Amerika all right! Drink, my friends, an' be happy!"

We drank and ate all we could hold. We talked to each other and listened to Sergei talk. And always I had a sad feeling that this was a time of departure — a sort of last supper after which we would all scatter to the four winds and life would change and there would never again be another supper at the home of Sergei Pushkin.

Because of this, it was the one evening of the year when I listened in a greedy sort of way to all that was happening and spoken around me, trying so hard to take in everything possible and never forget a word or gesture.

* * *

I can't help coming back to an old thought that eats away at me night and day. We did so much, and yet it was I who said, "No!" to borrowing more money to have Jim shipped home from England for burial here. It was I who said no, and it was they who suffered, for without knowing it myself then, I accused them for failing Jim, me and themselves.

If only Jim had not written what he thought that night — if only he stood beside the wall in Hammersmith and said, "I am here, fresh and ready to work. Nothing important happened before this — all that means anything is about to happen to me now!"

If only he'd said this and carried on with his studies and his almost child-like loves. But he tried to reach me, and it was a desperate thing to do. For he should have known the letter would come to me when the first snow was falling outside and mama was sitting in the chair you're in. She was patching over last year's clothes for the winter ahead. My old man was staring out the window, not having the guts to ask who the letter was from or what it said. He had his large, flat hands hooked behind his belt and he was thinking pretty deep, because his brows were crinkled up.

"What's wrong?" I asked her after I'd put the letter into the stove and watched it flare up. "Didn't we make any money this year that we're back on the same clothes we wore last year this time?"

"Sure we made money, kid — lots of money!" My old man said this with a short laugh, but he didn't look at me.

"Then it's gone out to Jim again — Rhodes scholarship or not. No one said it was gone so quick!"

Now he turned to me, and he was so mad one of his cheeks was jerking with a jumpy nerve.

"I don't want to hear another word about your brother, you hear me? Jim's going to make it up to us. A couple more years in school and there'll be more than just his picture in the papers — there'll be money to pay us back with — big money such as we never had a chance to make ourselves! You'll see I'm telling the truth! So don't talk nonsense! Better still, don't even think nonsense!"

100

We faced each other a long time — the father gone greedy on some kind of hope, and me, the son. Already the stone-picker, threatening brother-hatred as I killed land and brought it back to life with my hands and sunshine from the sky.

When had my boyhood gone, and when did the man take over in me? Forgetting was a wild horse, galloping away from me, taking on its back the memory of weeks without end when I kept to myself and felt beard grow and the heart become changed. I laughed sometimes, then and now, but not very much.

I remember laughing like hell watching Pete Wilson trying to sell my old man three sacks of flour at his store. All my old man wanted and could afford was one sack. Pete's gone now — the store where Sophie Makar met Freddy burned down, and Pete went south to set up a hardware business outside of Calgary. Pete and my old man never got along. After the fire, he started at least one story that damned near got Pete in trouble.

This story had it that Pete forgot he had to get out of the building, so when he was pouring coal oil all over his stock, he poured a mess right across the doorway. After he was supposed to have lit the match and got the fire started, he had one hell of a job finding where the door was and getting outside before getting himself trapped for good in there. My old man set this story going, saying he'd been walking past the store and saw Pete come out the door, kerosene tin in his hand and his clothes full of smoke.

"It's a damned lie!" Pete Wilson swore. "I've lost my business and someone's trying to ruin my insurance claim!"

It was a lie, because the day of the fire my old man and I were working together. He never saw Pete that day. And Pete Wilson didn't have his insurance claim ruined. His pigsty of a store was heavily insured. But I began telling about the sacks of flour . . .

"Take three sacks," Pete says to my old man. "Winter's

long, and it'll save you coming back when the snow is up to your earholes."

"One will do. I only got money for one sack of flour."

Pete Wilson chewed on a stray chunk of moustache that hung over his mouth and he looked my father over carefully. Like I say, there was no love between those two and this time both of them were ripe for a bit of argument. So it was starting.

"Hell, take three!" Pete goes on. "I'll give you credit. I'd give you half the store on your word, I trust you."

This was the kind of talk that got my old man going. He didn't mind being damned for his business dealings and he didn't mind praise. But when Pete Wilson started in with this praise that wasn't really praise, he started tugging his ear.

"What're you driving at?" he demanded. Pete shrugged.

"Nothing. I think you should take three bags of flour and save yourself bother later on."

"What's the point of going into debt when all I need is one damned sack of your flour? I came in here to buy a sack of flour, so if you can't sell it to me, say so and I'll go some place else!"

Which was just talk, because some place else was in town, and he wasn't going into town for a sack of flour that cost twenty cents more than what Pete was charging.

"Do whatever you like. I'm overstocked. Haven't got place to store too much flour without mice getting at it in a week or two. So take three bags and I'll throw in ten pounds of sugar for the same price." The store-keeper slammed his hand down on the counter as if he was throwing down a high card in a game. It sounded like a good deal, but because they couldn't agree on anything, my old man became more stubborn.

"Nope. When I need more flour, I'll come and get another sack!"

"Well," Pete slowly took out a cigarette and his eyes

crinkled with worry before he lit up. "Well, I hope so. But supposing you can't come back — you ever think of that?"

I saw my father's ears come up.

"What do you mean by that?" he wanted to know.

"What I was going to say was supposing you took sick and died — nothing like that will happen, of course. But just suppose it did. Imagine that you're a neighbour and it happened to him, not you. If you took sick and died, would you want your wife and boy to go hungry without flour? I'm not saying this will happen to you, only to a neighbour of yours!"

"All right! So you said already!" He had my old man with that one. "Stop that kind of talk, will you! Nobody's going to die tomorrow — not me, not any of my neighbours!"

"How can anyone say when he's going to die? You don't know and I don't know." Pete Wilson was smiling now and blowing smoke-rings into a shelf of peanut brittle. "Besides, if your wife's got to choose between going hungry and . . . well, remarrying. Look now, you can't blame a woman, can you? You know as well as I do that sometimes a woman has to do these things."

"What things?" My old man tried to make his voice threatening, but it didn't come off. Pete kept blowing smoke-rings.

"Why," he was talking lazily now as if speaking to nobody but himself, "she might even marry a lumberjack because of tough times. Just think — how would you like your wife to be screwed by a lumberjack because you didn't leave her any flour before you died?"

My old man bought the three sacks of flour, and as we drove home that afternoon he spoke only once to me. He said if I was to repeat a word of what went on at the store, he'd kick my ass up into my shoulders. I said I'd never tell, but I had to cough some to kill the laughing that was starting up inside of me.

* * *

So many men come and go. Only a short time ago I was a kid, and I never gave a thought to death. How could a man die whose eyes were on fire and whose arm muscles stood out high and sharp? Or who ate the way some of the men in our neighbourhood ate? A guy named MacDonald who lived close in used to eat with two hands — a slab of bread in one hand and a piece of meat in the other. First the meat, and then the bread. In between chewing he talked. He was hard, tough. His mouth was scarred and busted up from fighting.

"So I shoot this deer! It was as tall as a house. The biggest deer I've ever killed and it was a hundred years old, it was that tough. First night on the hunt I tried to eat it, but it wouldn't chew. So I boiled it for three hours. Still it would break your teeth. So I cut a chunk out of the shank — enough to make a good sized steak, and putting it over a log, I worked it over with the butt-end of my axe. Goddamn it, but it was like beating rubber! I worked it over until I began to sweat. Then I says to myself, this way I'd die of hunger on this hunt. Got to forget the deer and eat something else, or I'll use up more strength softening the meat than I get back from eating it!"

He stuffed his mouth with more bread, chewed for a moment, then continued.

"I said to hell with it, and ate a can of pork and beans."

"Don't remember you bringing a deer home from last year's hunt." My mother wasn't believing his story.

"No, I didn't. I buried it right out there in the bush. You think it'd rot being that tough?" he asked my old man.

"Don't know."

"What makes meat rot?" MacDonald took another bite

104

of the pickled ham he held. "Eh — what makes meat rot, you know?"

Nobody knew, so nobody said anything.

MacDonald did a bit of farming, and fall and winter he was out in the backwoods shooting anything that had meat on its bones and walked. He used to cut cordwood once, but he's been too old for that quite a few years now.

He had a son, Sammy, who was a year older than I and about thirty pounds heavier. The guy was a bully, shoving smaller kids over with a bunt of his shoulder. He was always eating prunes and dribbling out the pits over his shirt front. In a lot of ways he resembled a young pig. I tried not to have any mix-ups with him.

Then one day we were playing tag in school and he was around. I caught him when he stopped near the schoolyard fence to dig up some prunes from his pocket. I tagged him.

"Beat it!" he hollered at me.

"You're it!" I shouted and waved at the others to run. He hauled off and hit me across my lips, making my front teeth bleed. At first I was too scared to do anything. Then he came at me and knocked me down with his shoulder and I started to cry. This was way back when I was a kid still in school.

"What the hell you crying for, you baby?" By now he was mad and scared himself. Instead of leaving me alone, he was so scared he started to kick me. The school bell rang then, ending our recess. Instead of going back to school, I got up and went home. My mother wanted to know what was the matter, and I told her I fell on my face and was sick.

When Jim got home that evening, he told the folks I had run away from school and that Sammy MacDonald was tattled on for hitting me and got strapped before the class. My old lady was all ready to go over to the MacDonald farm right then and complain to Sammy's old man about Sammy. But I kept shouting at her not to, and finally she made out like she wouldn't do it that day, but if it ever happened again, it would be a different story.

Sammy didn't take the strapping like any gentleman. I didn't expect him to. The next morning he came part way up the road to meet me. I was walking to school with Jim, and when he saw Sammy coming like that, Jim turned around and high-tailed it back home. I couldn't run. I wasn't going to run. But I was scared.

"You told the teacher on me!" Sammy said when he got to where I was standing. He spat out two prune pits.

"I didn't so tell."

"You did too. Bet you laughed when I got the strap!"

"I was home," I admitted kind of weakly.

"Chicken-shit!" But he didn't wait for a reply to that. He hit me across the mouth again like he'd done the day before. I fell and reached for my cap to put back on my head before I tried to get up. He took it out of my hand and threw it across the road. And while I tried to rub the tears out of my eyes, he walked over to the cap and with his back to me peed into it. I grabbed for a stone and threw it at him, then ran off the road along a cowpath, thinking I could lose him in the heavy bush.

But there was no losing Sammy. Fat and big as he was, he was fast on his feet. Soon I heard him panting just behind me. Then I fell, tearing my cheek open on a rose-bush that grew wild beside the path.

It might've been the cut, or maybe I was scared enough to do anything by now, but next thing I remember is kneeling beside Sammy, clubbing him over the head with a chunk of alder root. He wasn't moving now, and there was blood coming out of one of his ears.

"Say you got enough! Say it!" I was shouting at him. He didn't move or make a sound.

"PLEASE say it!"

Then I threw the root away and tried to lift him up, but he weighed a ton. I left him then and kept walking, sometimes running. I didn't sit down until I was by the river, and here I ate my carrot-jam sandwich which I carried behind my shirt, drinking down some river water after I'd eaten. I waited until dark before I turned home. Nobody seemed to notice me arriving. I told my mama I didn't want supper and went to bed.

I dreamed Sammy's father came to our house. I saw him talking to my folks in the dream. They talked so low nobody could hear what was said, but once in a while all of them turned to look at me, so I knew they were talking about my fight with Sammy. Then I dreamed they all came towards me, their faces angry.

"You killed Sammy!" MacDonald said like it didn't matter, but he had to do what was to be done.

I thought I shouted at him that I didn't mean it, but I'm not sure. Then the three of them, MacDonald, my old man and old lady, took me out of the house into the barn and hung me from a girder beam.

Anyway, what I started to say was that since those days, MacDonald has more or less given up his winter hunting, because he's had a bad run of rheumatics. Sammy went to a trade school where he learned to weld and got himself a job in a garage in Vegreville or some place near there.

No, I didn't hurt him all that bad. He was pretty sick for a few days after our fight, but we never tangled again. We didn't play or speak to one another either. Sometimes I'd turn quickly and see him watching me from a distance, as if trying to figure something out. And there were times I stood watching him, remembering him lying on the path. Only I stopped looking at him this way, because it made me shiver.

* * *

There's always been dancing at Anderson's Hall. Summers back there were three guys — one with a guitar, the other with a fiddle and a third with a drum — came all the way from Clyde every second Saturday to play a dance here. They brought half the crowd with them, and the hall used to get so packed you'd have to drink your coffee standing up when the lunch break came. My folks decided to go a few times, but they weren't used to so many people they didn't know, so they stopped going. It was tough for them to understand that because most everybody owned a car outside of this area after the war, people were moving farther, faster. They sort of looked upon the outsider coming here to dance as someone out to have a wild time where he wasn't known. There were wild times, but it was we who made them.

I got into the back seat of a car with three guys I knew who'd come in from the lumber camps. We drank gin out of a bottle, and the four of us got so drunk we all passed out in a heap back of the hall. Next morning old man Anderson himself found us and gave us holy hell for being stupid.

Before I forget, one other reason my folks didn't come dancing was because Marta Walker started coming alone. Not only my mother, but other married women as well, stared at her as if she didn't belong, but she stayed. For the first few dances she mostly stood back along the wall, watching us. Some were kids who'd been students of her's in school. She didn't seem to want to do any dancing or anything, just stand there and look. So the next time the three lumberjack friends of mine and I got drinking, we dared one of the boys to go ask Marta to dance. Hector braced himself with a stiff drink and went, and she danced with him.

The rest of us watched from near the door. We giggled when they didn't break apart after the first dance, but kept on dancing again. This time they were talking a little bit to one another. Two weeks later, Hector asked her without us daring, and this time he danced four dances with her.

During lunch at midnight, they went outside together and I sort of snooped around but couldn't find them.

"Where you been with that woman?" I asked Hector when the dancing started up again and he came back. Hector looked right past me and his mouth was shut tight and stayed shut tight. I asked again.

"Keep your dirty nose out of my business," he said.

"I'm not interested in your business. You can do what you want with her. You can even . . ." He looked at me now, his fist brought up and his eyes hot and wild.

That romance built up steam pretty quickly. To get from Anderson's Hall to here, the quickest way is across Eric Walker's farm. I ordinarily chose the longer way, following the road, because Walker had this damned German Shepherd dog that would just as soon take your leg off as sleep. I didn't hear talk of him bothering the neighbours, but one night after a dance I took a short-cut through Eric's yard and the dog came out of nowheres and had me down and shouting, and I decided to stay away from walking this way again. I would've too.

But Nancy Burla came to the dance with a couple of nurses one time. One of the nurses had a boyfriend with a car, and as I stood in the stagline, I looked up and saw her smiling at me. Meeting her outside the hospital like this threw me. Instead of letting my surprise come and go, I had to try and cover it by being smart-alecky.

"Didn't know you danced," I said to her. "Didn't even think you could walk very good!"

The smile faltered on her face and she got beet-red. One of the nurses with her giggled. I hated myself when I did these things. It was a thing with my nerves. When I get excited in a happy sort of way, I say the damnedest things to people. I want to stop myself when I hear me saying them, but I can't. Nancy moved away from where I stood, and soon I saw her dancing with one of the boys who'd come from Clyde. I sat and watched and felt miserable.

Yet when the dance ended she came over and sat by me and I couldn't think of anything to say to her. So I kept my mouth shut, which was as well for it kept me from insulting her. She seemed to understand how I felt, for when the next dance was played, she got up the same time I did and we danced without me asking her to. She smelled of sweet perfume and woman's soap, and her hands were warm and moist. With my hand over the back of her dress, I could feel her back muscles, firm and tugging as we moved across the floor. I felt sad and happy all at the same time. When the dance finished for the night, I walked to the car which had brought her and the other nurses.

"So awright — so give 'im a kiss an' let's go!" The loud-mouth who owned the car rolled down his window to tease her. The crazy things I do — without holding myself back, I pulled her to me and kissed her on the mouth, and her friends looking on. Then I turned away and went home, blind, because my eyes were full of tears and I couldn't stop them coming.

I wanted to reach home quickly and get into bed so I could dream of a different kind of life, with Nancy Burla beside me. A house of my own. A few chickens and some meadow with a cow that had enough to eat and give milk on. We'd get by on very little. People can, and do.

One of the few times my old man and I could talk and understand each other was when we talked about farm people — peasants, and how nothing could break them.

"Give a man like you or me a shovel and a bit of dirt and he'll grow grub no matter what happens — atomic bombs or no!" he'd say proudly, and I knew he was right. People born generations to earth know about seed, water and sun without being told. They can suffer the kind of pain that sends a city-bred man to suicide, and they come out of it a little more bent and wrinkled, but still doing those things that give food and shelter to themselves and their children.

110

Not that I like this. I'd give all this away a thousand times over for a year of the kind of joy I know a man can have. Sometimes I feel I can see Jim as clear as if his soul and heart were made of glass, and everything inside was written out to be read. He's saying to me: "I don't hate you. I love you. I'll never be older than you. But I've seen so much I would show you if I could. It came too soon for me and too much. I'm a child . . . you'll have to care for me!"

And then I cry. Believe me, man — I drop my head down and cry. I cry for every goddamned day I've spent here, rooted to a hundred and sixty acres of mud, rock and bush. I cry for Jim and not hearing *his* story before he decided there'd never be anyone to hear him. I cry because I've lost her, and with her gone, I've lost life itself. I'm not even as useful as a second-hand tractor you can buy for two hundred dollars. I cost more to keep and I can't do as much work. I thought once I'd write a long poem where I'd tell everything. Or make up a cowboy song to sing. But the words never came. I've stood for hours out there in the field, the wind blowing all around me, drying the soil and sapping the water out of my flesh. I've felt it all, but could never tell others how it felt.

That night I left her I wanted to get home as quickly as possible. I crossed Eric Walker's barley-field and began walking through his yard as quietly as I could so's not to surprise the dog. The house was dark. The path in front of me was dark. Marta had been at the dance, again dancing with Hector a lot of the time, but I didn't see her when the dance finished. Neither did I see Hector.

Even before I heard her giggle and sigh, I knew they were near me, making love. I stopped in the middle of the Walker yard and looked around. Darkness was cut only by the stars. Then I knew where they where. Over in the feed-shed by the barn. The door of the shed was open, and I heard Marta laugh again and Hector pleading with her.

111

I forgot about the dog and my fear of him. I began to hurry away, my footsteps kicking up pebbles, but I was too shamed and excited to care how much noise I made in my retreat. Then I stopped, wanting to steal over to the shed and spy on them, to share by listening to them in their sinful pleasure. No — I mustn't! I had to run away from here. Then my foot kicked the dog and I fell over him.

I was on my feet in a flash and ready to protect myself. But nothing happened. I knelt beside him and reached out to touch him. He was still warm and wet. I touched him again, this time exploring. When I found the hot hole in his ribs I almost became sick. After coming here they had to kill the dog to have each other.

And in the dark house, Eric Walker, who never laughed, was having himself a good sleep.

* * *

There is the palm and the back of the hand. And so it is with a community. Some are known for the work they do, others for the way they can enjoy themselves. Let me tell you about a woman who could dance a whole story she could tell no other way.

Elizabeth Junco was her name, but I grew up knowing her by her first name. As I suppose my folks did before me. You go three miles towards town down this road. At three miles you turn off and go another mile towards the river. This last mile is hardly more than a footpath, and at the end of the path is Elizabeth's place.

She's about seventy now, but smart as a whip. She's never changed. Always grey-haired, skin parched and brown, and hands that are thin and small as a kid's. Her clothes don't have any colour or shape to them any more, she's worn the same things so long now. Winter and summer she's got the same skirt and jacket on, with wads of other clothing underneath. But she can bake an apple pie like

112

nobody else can bake an apple pie here. And she smokes a pipe.

If you ask her why, she'll say, "For me asthma."

We have farmers' picnics every year on the school playground. In the old days, neighbours walked to the picnic, carrying kids on their shoulders. Now they drive in, with their cars and half-ton trucks all washed and waxed for the day. But they get dusty fast, and there's always a few brats moving around drawing pumpkin heads with crazy mouths over the dust that's settled on the waxed metal. Some write dirty words, but that's only some, and I chase them away myself when I see them ready to write.

Anyhow — at the picnics they've always had a baking contest. My old lady took the best bread prize two years in a row. For prizes, she once got that set of glassware you can see up there on the shelf. The second time she got a cushion cover, but that's long gone.

Every year Elizabeth brought her apple pie, and every year she's taken a prize. You've never seen apple pie like the one she bakes. Rich, thick, spiced so you can smell it a mile off, and covered with whipped cream this thick! It makes your mouth water just to see it stand on the table during the judging. I once had a small spoon of it after the judging, and it was something to remember! It got so no woman brought pies to put against the one Elizabeh entered. Part of this was a dislike the women felt for Elizabeth. For after all this old woman lived without a man or means and beat them at their own game.

Elizabeth had hardly enough land for a garden, at the back of which was a tiny shack and a clothes-line. Next to the shack, planted in such a way that it could be covered with a big canvas sheet attached to the roof for winter, was a small sour-apple tree. It was the small green apples she got from this tree that she baked the pies out of. That was all — no cattle, no dog or cat. My old lady knew how poorly Elizabeth lived, and one summer she tried to pull a dirty one on her at the picnic. When a crowd of women were standing around, she says to Elizabeth:

"Tell me, dearie, with no cows of your own, how do you manage to get whipped cream? If you tried to bring it from town, or even from another farm, surely it'd sour before you got it home! But there's a pasture meadow near your place . . . and Russel Jones keeps four milk cows there now . . . I wonder if it's possible you might be milking one of these cows when nobody was looking!"

My mama had no right doing that. A kid could figure out Elizabeth was stealing milk for cream to cover her pie, but it didn't have to be talked about with the old woman standing there.

"Now what makes you think that's the kind of dirty work I'd do, huh? Or have you seen me doing it?" she asked my mother quietly, then she continued: "You surprise me, Josie — all dressed up so nice and thinkin' such thoughts of other people less lucky than you!"

My old lady did feel ashamed. It served her right to have her nose put out of joint for what she tried to do.

"Oh, forget it!" she said. Old Elizabeth wasn't going to let her off that easy though.

"Forget what? You telling these good women that I'm a thief?"

"I didn't say any such thing! I'd never think of it, and if you think I said it, I'm sorry."

Elizabeth smiled and looked squarely at my mother.

"I'm sure glad of that, Josie, an' no hard feelings," she said. "You're such a fine, upstanding woman, with a good man an' two boys of your own. Always somebody around to see to you and take care of you. That's nice."

She looked around as if wanting the judging to be over and done with quickly.

"If they don't come to judge, I'm invitin' you ladies to have the pie with me," Elizabeth grinned and began packing her pipe. When the judges did come up to choose the best baking that summer, Elizabeth again got first prize for her pie.

Eilizabeth was there every time when they held regular dances at Anderson's Hall. She never stayed the whole night because she wouldn't light her pipe for fear of offending someone in a closed building. A few dances to get things going, and she'd be gone. When she danced, it was like lecturing us not to forget there was more to living than stones, barley and debts.

She was like a deer on her feet. When every man who'd dance with her got too tired to go on, and no fresh ones came forward, they would clear the floor and old Elizabeth went at it alone — holding her skirts like a girl, and her legs moving so fast it made you dizzy watching her.

"Turkey in the straw — fast!" If the orchestra didn't know the music, they had to come in with as good a tune quickly, or they'd be booed off the stage.

Now there were handclaps in time to the music. And in the middle of the big floor was Elizabeth, her white hair flying and her mouth slightly open with pure joy in the music and speed of the dance. Applause, and some man from the back of the hall shouting, "Bravo, Elizabeth!"

Another would shout from nearer to her, "If it wasn't for a wife and five kids already, I'd run away with you tonight, that's for sure!"

The music played on, but she stopped, brushing down her threadbare clothing over her thin old body and looking down at herself. Faint droplets of sweat made her forehead and cheeks shine. There'd be some laughter among the women, and Elizabeth would look up at the man in front of her and say:

"Shame on you for even thinking such thoughts — with a wife and five kids of your own! You ought to be ashamed."

The man would argue back that he meant it, and devil take the consequences. But would she dance some more?

Elizabeth shook her head as if to say it wasn't the same any more — not until the next time. As the dancing started up again, with younger people coming on the floor, Elizabeth would pull her clothes more snugly around her and leave to walk home all by herself.

* * *

We had a grey cat called Mike, who sat and slept on the chair you're on. Can't say for sure if he came to us as a kitten, or if he was born right on the property from one of the strays that came and went. He seemed to have been with us for years, and always boss of the barnyard. Cows stepped aside when he came down the path from the house to the barn. I'm not surprised, because even I gave him the road when we met. There was something wise and firm about the way he walked and held his head. Like if he was a man, you'd call him "sir" without thinking. He earned his respect as far as the family was concerned, because Mike was a good mouser and kept our cellar and granaries free of mice and squirrels.

In the house, the chair you're in was his to sit or sleep in. Nobody ever thought of lifting him out. Partly because Mike left the farm once in a while. Four times in all he was gone for as long as eight months.

Each time he went, we were sure he was gone for good, especially since nobody in the neighbourhood saw or heard of him. It's easy to lose a cat in the bush around here. A weasel or cougar could kill him. Or if he was able to survive wild animals, he could easily freeze to death in winter, when temperatures can drop to forty below-zero and worse for weeks at a time. Then one spring or summer morning when you'd almost forgotten him, Mike would be there on the porch, sunning himself and yawning when you picked him up!

We made a lot of him on his returns. He got plenty of

fresh milk, and if we'd slaughtered pork, mama would fry a bit of liver for him to eat. Jim and I played and patted him a lot for a few days until we were sure he understood how much he'd been missed.

But each time Mike came back, he was changed in a way that shocked us. The same kind of changes you'd likely get with old soldiers who go from one war to the next, or saints who take it on themselves to tame a fierce world and never quite make it.

The first time, part of his right ear was missing, and the tip of his tail had frozen or been bitten off. The next time he took off, he came back with his left ear completely off and part of a front paw torn off by a trap. The third time, all the hair off one side of his stomach was gone, showing a large patch of white, dry skin. The fourth time, he lost one eye.

I took it on myself to save him from more damage, by taking him inside the house at nights and closing all the windows to keep him in. For I felt the next time he left, he would not return. There was only a small part of old Mike left then, and the spirit of a cat is no stronger than the spirit of a man.

I was right. For he took off in broad daylight once and never did come back.

* * *

Have you ever heard of Calling Lake?

It's only an hour and a half by car when the roads are dry. When there wasn't a proper road ten years ago, it took us a day to get there by sled and horse in winter. For every winter some of us went to Calling Lake to fish through the ice. If you were low on money, one way to keep a family fed was to fall back on fish and potatoes in the winter.

One winter I drove out with Wally Pantaluk, who was at that time one of the strongest men around. He was short and solid muscled. I think he was about twice my age then, but he could still break ice and pull in a net with the strength of two men.

We got to the lake as it was turning dark. By what light was left and the help of a bonfire on the beach, we sank our nets and had supper and warm tea before rolling in under blankets and hay on the sled to sleep. With the first grey of morning, we were pulling the net out of the thin channel in the ice.

It was cold, but we had to work fast to dump the heavy catch of whitefish and pickerel before they froze into the net once it was lifted out of the water. Our mitts crackled with ice. Our breath froze in white puffs as we panted with the strain, and soon the sun was up, but it gave no warmth. We were almost finished now, and I began rolling up the net while Wally took out the last few fish. He was drenched with water from the net and from his own perspiration.

"Hey — boy! Get this done and we take five! I feel like I'm on fire!" he shouted to me over his shoulder. Then he tossed up the last fish on the snow and stood up.

"I'll fold the net myself," I said to him. "You go on the sled and rest."

"The way I feel the last place I want to rest is the sled. I'm gonna lay me down right here and cool off first!"

He began to settle down on the ice, and I started feeling afraid.

"Don't lay on the ice, Wally! You'll catch cold!"

He grinned at me.

"When Wally Pantaluk gets hot, Wally Pantaluk has to cool down before he can work some more! Leave the fish to freeze hard. I'll help you load them right away."

He was still looking at me as he stretched out on a spot of ice that was windswept bare. He lay on his right side, his head resting on his hand. In five minutes a small pool of water had formed under him. When he rose, I saw that he staggered a little as he came to the sled where I'd been loading the half-frozen fish. The colour was gone from his face. He had himself a cup of coffee we'd kept warm in a jar wrapped in newspaper, as I harnessed the horses to the sled. When I was done and had the net tied down to the back of the sled, Wally climbed slowly to his seat, wrapping himself in a blanket while I put up our food box. He shivered a lot as we drove back home.

That was the end of Wally Pantaluk as a workman. Even as we drove in, he suddenly took a scare of something only he felt or knew, and he whimpered and shivered like that all the way. I asked him what was wrong, but he wouldn't talk. When I happened to look into his face, I noticed his eyes had gone bloodshot and were running tears.

I got around to visiting him once at his home that winter. He'd lost a lot of weight, and was laying in bed smelling powerful strong of mustard and camphor. By spring he was up and around, but it was as if the side on which he had lain on the ice had shrunk on him. He walked bent over in that direction. He wasn't able to turn his head without shuffling his whole body around. And he couldn't walk without a stick. He tried to put in his own crop on his farm that spring, then ended up hiring men to do it for him.

The winter following, Wally got married. His woman was older than he by quite a few years and she had this real heavy moustache on her lip, so I don't think he was very happy.

* * *

Some of the other things that happened you already know. My old lady got her first stroke in time for Christmas — she was in hospital a month then, and that ended our Christmas that year and every year after.

A young kid called Steve Swanson came from Edmonton and paid a two year lease on an acre of land just downhill from the garden right on this farm. He built himself a shack. After he left, we kept the shack open a while, thinking he'd come back. When he didn't come, we finally turned it into a chicken coop.

But first, you'll want to know about my mother's stroke. When we heard of Jim's death it didn't come through to us for a while. Being killed in a motorcycle crash — at high-speed, in England? You know the way it felt? It seemed like so far away and such an unlikely way for Jim to go after all these years of books and schools, that I really think we believed it wasn't Jim at all. It was a mistake and somebody else got killed and we'd hear the true story in an hour or two. But when I tuned in to the radio and they repeated what the telegram from his school said over the news, we knew then.

My old lady just kept puttering around the stove.

"Well, what the hell do we say to all that? What the hell do we say?" My father was sitting over there when I shut the radio off, and he muttered and then whacked the table with his fist.

Then Dan Makar came, bringing another telegram from town. He left after saying how sorry he was about Jim, and my old man opened the new telegram. It was from Jim's student fraternity, saying he'd requested they bury him through some insurance they had for this sort of thing in his school. But if we wanted Jim's body home, then —

"Yes, we must!" My old lady dropped a saucepan on the stove as she turned. My father nodded and got to his feet. He was on the way to the bedroom to change.

"What're you doing?" I asked.

"Changing to go into town, boy," he said. "See if we can raise more money to bring Jim home and bury him."

"From the bank?" I wanted to know.

"What's it to you? You finished cleaning the barn and doing your chores for the day? Get on with it!" Suddenly he got hard and mean with me, not really attacking, but defending himself in a way that hurt me worse than him. Maybe if I hadn't done this I would have let all this go. But I felt an anger — hot and wicked — shaping up inside me, edging closer to an explosion. My mother moved to the table and sat down.

"Your father knows what he's doing . . ." she began to say.

"No!" I shouted at him. "You're not borrowing a damned penny more and that's that!"

"Stop it — both of you!" my old lady whimpered. He stood glaring at me for a moment, then came over quick and slapped me hard. I kept watching him and saw his eyes look away with shame. Then we heard her fall off the chair and the fight ended.

We stood over her for maybe five minutes, both of us thinking she wasn't lying there — we were both imagining it. Then we came to life — I, running for the barn to get horses and sled for taking her to hospital, and he sponging her head with vinegar and pleading with her to forgive all and live.

We learned all the bad news about her soon's we got her into the hospital. On the way home, the old man asked me to wait while he went into the liquor store.

At home that night, he sat up by himself after I went to bed and got himself blind drunk. He staggered into my room towards morning, mumbling about us understanding each other. By the time I was awake enough to raise myself up in bed, he'd gone to sleep sitting on the edge. I put him down, covered him, and got dressed to begin the day three hours earlier than usual.

* * *

Steve Swanson had four toes to each foot. He never drank water from a well. In summer he caught rain-water, and in winter he melted down snow to make his soup and tea.

He was only a year or two older than me, and he could play a fiddle like nobody I'd ever heard play before. Not just dance tunes, but heavier stuff also. Opera and things like that.

"Where'd you learn all that kind of stuff, Steve?" I asked when we first worked on his shack. My old man charged him forty dollars a year for lease of an acre of land, and I thought that was high if a man was also to build a place for himself to live in. So I helped Steve put up his eight-by-twelve foot frame but, wondering all the time why he came from Edmonton to live like this.

"From records. I played records and learned by ear."

He showed me the box of records he'd brought with him. He also brought a record player to play them on, but it was no use to him here for it had to have electric power to work. If he'd lived here now he could've carried the player to one of the farms where they've got power. But when Steve was here, the powerline was still about fifteen miles away and any farm wanting power had to have eleven hundred dollars to shell out in advance. Eleven hundred dollars is more than a farm such as this can produce in the best year, and there hasn't been a best year since I've lived here. And even if you got that much, you'd still have to pay off taxes, seed, fertilizer, repairs to machinery — and in my case, hospital bills and loan repayments, plus some for her missionary work among the bums, and what'd be left.

But Steve — yes . . . I asked him finally what made him come out here. He didn't say a word, but picked up his fiddle and started tuning it. After a while he looked as if he was going to put it down.

"A woman?" I asked.

He picked up the fiddle again and started playing "Buffalo Girls" and stamping his stockinged foot on the rough plank floor we'd put into the shack. That was the first time I saw his feet and noticed something peculiar about them. They were pointed and long at the toe.

"How come?" I touched his foot with my boot and immediately felt foolish for doing it.

"Four toes." And he stopped playing and pulled off a sock to show me. "Ever seen a guy with four toes before?"

I said I hadn't and he laughed. Then we got back to work finishing the door and setting in his window, for the first snow had fallen and the wind could turn icy within hours this late in the year.

It was a few weeks later and well into cold weather when I saw Steve again — just around Christmas it was. I saw Eric Walker drive over to his shack after the last heavy snow to deliver a bigger stove. And a few times I saw Steve going out axe in hand to cut up a bit of fallen log for firewood. I'd always stop in the barnyard to listen to him chop wood with the short "chick-chick" axe blows of a city man!

I was milking cows one evening by lantern light in the barn when Steve came in to see me. I never heard him open the barn door, because my old man was giving me enough worries to think about, and when Steve touched me on the shoulder, I almost come off the milking stool with surprise.

"What the hell's the matter with you, creeping up on a guy like that?"

My father was getting just about useless since my mother's stroke, and I didn't know what to do about him. He started drinking pretty heavily. He got another bottle of whisky from town the next time we drove in to see her. When he drank that, he went out once on foot and came back with a gallon jug of moonshine he'd got some place in the neighbourhood. Drink wasn't making him any happier. For one thing, he didn't eat much any more. For another, it started to make him turn grey. The month the old lady was away sick, he became an old man, and that's no lie. I was too busy keeping the place going single-handedly to stop and figure out why everything was going to pot. Jim was buried in England by now, and as far as I know, my father never even got around to replying to the second telegram. I started the whole mess moving this way, but at that time I couldn't see further than the next chore so the guilt didn't come until later — half a year later.

Anyway, Steve scared the hell out of me.

"I didn't mean to. Sorry." He shuffled around a little beside me before asking, "You think old Anderson would let me play dances at his hall?"

I'd told Steve some time earler about the dances, and how Anderson often took different players in for music.

"I don't know," I said. "Why don't you go over and ask him tomorrow?"

"I'd rather you asked him for me."

"What the hell! It's your problem — if you want to play, go talk to Anderson. I've enough to do around here. Besides, how can you play a dance with just a fiddle? You've got to find someone to play guitar with you."

"I can't just go up to him and say I play a violin good! It'd be better if you told him!" Steve looked like he was making to go out and not say any more to me. But he stopped, but didn't look at me.

"I've no money," he said quietly. "I'm broke, and I've only got grub to last a week an' no more!"

I didn't believe him. He said it so straight out that I was sure he was having me on.

"Tough!" I said, and started to laugh. He sort of let out a groan, and before I could speak to him again, he'd left the barn and was gone in the night. Next morning, I went over to see him at his shack, but he was gone, and a nail had been driven into the frame of the door to keep it shut.

Week after Christmas — second of January, my old lady was ready to come out of hospital. My old man cut out the booze all New Year's Day and had himself a bath. Except for being thin and grey, he seemed more cheerful than I'd seen him the month before. But we hadn't talked, and now it was hard to begin. So we loaded up blankets and two hot water bottles into the sleigh and drove into town with hardly a word said. It was just before noon when we got in, the time the old doctor would be gone for lunch. There was a new doctor in town — he'd come from Australia, but when my mother went in, he was up north, so she had the same Doctor Brent who'd operated on my ulcer a year before. Because he was in the hospital the afternoons a person could visit, I didn't see my old lady during the month she was in. I hung around the pool-hall and Chinese cafe while my father went to her.

Before we could get mama out, the old man had to sign forms and arrange how he'd pay. I paced around the front office and next thing I was in the corridor and headed to the ward where Nancy would be at this hour. I hadn't seen her for a few months — no, less than that — six weeks! But I was older by a year now, supporting a sick mother and a father who was turning to putty on me. I had to stop in the corridor and take a deep breath to catch up with myself — to know what to tell her. An older nurse who was big as a house came over to me and asked what I wanted. I told her.

"Miss Burla isn't working here any longer. She's with Doctor Helsen now, working in his office."

"The new doctor?"

She nodded and then herded me back to the front of the building. My mother was down now, thin and rattly as a ghost, but smiling from where she sat on a bench waiting for me. I kissed her and then we led her out.

Our horses snorted steam on the winter air. As we drove away the sleigh runners squealed on the frozen snow. The Christmas lights were still up in town, some of them staying lit right through the day.

"What did you men do over the holiday?" Mama asked in a tired voice.

"Nothing," I said.

"Nothing," the old man repeated and looked away from me, for I wondered if he'd tell her about his drinking. I think she knew, for after we were out of town he gave me the reins to drive and himself bent down to kiss her. When his mouth touched hers, I saw her eyes flutter open with surprise.

"You going to live now, Josie. I was scared you wouldn't." He kept saying that over and over to her, like he still wasn't sure it was so. She didn't say anything back to him. When we got home I lifted her off the sleigh and carried her in. Her breath smelled of hospital, and when I was putting her down and she reached up to hold my neck and help steady herself, her hands were icy cold.

Affairs didn't improve between my old man and myself. Even with her back home, we still couldn't get around to speaking again. He had his odd shot of whisky with tea now, but he did cut back on what he'd drunk during the time she was away. But the strangest change was in her. She'd somehow become very resigned and quiet. She was still too weak to get up, but she didn't seem to mind the filth filling up the house, and once when we missed a meal, she didn't mention it to the old man or me.

What really threw me was to see John the wife-beater now turned evangelist stopping by. It'd been years since he'd come around, and that was during the time he was bad. This time it wasn't the old man he came to see, but her. While we hung around the kitchen, drinking tea and wondering what the hell was going on, John went into the bedroom where she was and stayed talking to her for about an hour. When he left, I looked in and saw he'd left her lap full of his magazines and little religious booklets.

"Is she — taking religion?" I whispered to my father. He

looked past me as he lifted his shoulders in the most weary shrug.

"Who cares?" he said.

Steve came back two weeks later. I heard his violin one morning as I was busy carrying hay off the stack into the barn to feed some cows which were due to calve shortly. It was a clear, frosty morning, and the fiddle sound carried right into the barn. He was playing his heavy music. I finished feeding quickly and went over to see him. He wore a new suit, and had a nice sheepskin hat on his head. He had his feet on a stool in front of the blazing stove and played with his eyes closed. When I came in, he jumped up.

"Close that door, stupid peasant!" he shouted at me. "You're putting me out of tune!"

I'd brought in a cloud of icy air with me, which kept billowing in as I tried to kick my rubber overboots off, holding the door open because I couldn't keep my mind on two things at one time. He put his fiddle on the bed and covered it with a pillow.

"Close the door!"

"I'm sorry about laughing when you asked for money," I said.

"I never asked for money!"

"Well, you know, when you were broke and wanted me to talk to Anderson about playing!"

"Forget it. I've got all kinds of money." He took out a roll from his pocket. There must've been a couple hundred in it. By now the shack was warm again, and he took the fiddle out and started playing, but something was worrying him, because he couldn't play more than a few notes without going off. I hung around, but he only sat with a long look on his face and his fiddle on his lap, so I went back to my work.

Like I told you, Steve paid two years lease and put this shack up. But he didn't stay out that first winter. Next time the old man and I were in town to shop the mountie stopped us on the street.

"You got a guy called Swanson living at your place?" he asked. We said yes, and asked what was wrong. The mountie said he wasn't sure, and walked away without saying anything more.

When we got home, we saw the door of Steve's shack hanging open and no sign of Steve. I ran over and found some of his stuff still there, except for his clothes and his fiddle. The records in the box were busted, and he'd put the axe through the middle of the record player, so there was nothing left except the stove, a half dozen pocketbooks and the bed and bedding, and two small cooking pots and spoons.

My old man came in then and looked the place over.

"The kid say anything about being in trouble?" he asked me.

"He needed money once."

"You give him some?"

"No."

He gave me a sad, long smile.

"Too bad you didn't," he said, and walked out.

I talked to the mountie about Steve, and was told he'd got six months for theft in Edmonton. So I took his stuff out and put it in a corner of the back porch in case he comes back to collect it. Then I made a chicken-coop out of the shack.

* * *

It was early June — spring. The crops were in the ground and winter-born calves were as full of devil as seven-year-old children. Much work of picking stones off the fields had to be done. At home, an unreal kind of happiness was driving my mother to John's evangelical meetings, and my father had gotten as thin and bug-eyed as a man with a killing disease. I now knew he was being driven by some secret worry he wasn't telling about. He drank openly as he had when she was away, but he was never drunk.

One day I got so damned sad I couldn't go on working. Blackbirds walked beside me like they knew what was going on in my head and heart. I had to get out and see her — tell her, or if I got nervous and said things I didn't mean, make her look at me and understand.

She was working for this Doctor Helsen, the fellow I told you about, who'd come from Australia last fall. During a farm union meeting for the whole region, they said he came out to speak about state-controlled medicine for everyone. I wasn't at the meeting, but Sergei Pushkin said the doctor stood for the farmer and worker, and we could learn a lot from him. Word was also going around that he and Doctor Brent weren't hitting it off too well at the hospital because Doctor Helsen wasn't charging anywhere near the old fees for visits and surgery.

He'd been away when my mother had her stroke, so he hadn't treated her. But I'd seen him around town, and liked what I saw. He was a big guy, sandy-haired and with this voice that sounded like a deep horn down inside his stomach.

I walked into town, dressed just the way I was coming off the fields and so goddarned sad I didn't know which way to turn. It was a long walk and I got in just before lunch. I hadn't seen Nancy Burla to talk to going on eight or nine months. She seemed both surprised and happy to have me walk into the new office this Doctor Helsen had. There were two other people waiting to see the doctor.

"How are you, Nancy? I . . . want to see you by yourself," I said to her.

"Is there anything wrong with you?" she asked, and she was worried.

"No, no! But I don't know if there is or isn't!" I felt the two women waiting for the doctor looking at me with

129

the blank stares of farmers who hear every word and don't forget a thing. "Can we . . ."

I pointed to the drugstore across the street. She smiled at the two women and came from behind the desk. She'd gotten thinner than she'd been at the hospital and there was a slight slouch to her shoulders.

"But only a minute. Doctor Helsen will be back any time."

In the drugstore, a few high school kids were reading comics and magazines at the rack. A little girl with a twisted shoulder and dressed in white, as Nancy was dressed, brought us coffee at the bar, then hung around, looking at me without seeming to. I wanted her to go away, but she wouldn't.

"I've only a minute." Nancy spoke, then looked up at the girl of the bar. "How are tricks today, Sadie?"

"Fine."

"Nancy, I want to say something to you, so will you listen . . ." I started off that way, and felt wretched as hell because it was all going wrong.

"Well?" She was looking at me now, laughter in her eyes. First laughter, then anger, for the little bitch back of the bar giggled.

"I don't know what I'll do — unless you marry me!"

It was out, and in such a loud, fast voice I could hear the students at the magazine rack crumple their magazines to listen for more. I wanted to run from the place, but I couldn't move off the stool. Sweat was trickling down the sides of my face, and I felt like some grimy, sweaty, smelly-armpitted joker grunting at the slaughter table. My hand was bigger than the cup I held, but the cup was too heavy to keep up and I spilled hot coffee over my wrist before I dropped it. A long shudder went through Nancy. Her eyes turned away, shocked, and she put down her coffee very carefully. When she spoke, her voice was so soft only I could hear her.

130

"It's not going to be. A year ago, maybe. But now you're crazy to ask. It's not going to be!"

"But I love you, and I thought . . ."

"It doesn't matter!" She was on her feet now. "What's love anyhow? You think I don't know how it'd be? Smarten up! Just kids and tough times . . . my old man's a drunk because of it — I ever tell you how much of a drunk he is?"

She was gone out the door, her legs knotted like those of a runner. Outside the door, she did run across the street. Before she turned away, I saw her face once through the window. She brushed away at her eyes with both hands and then she started running. The waitress giggled again and took my cup away.

Then one day my old man says to me, "That Doc Helsen got married — anyone tell you? Married the nurse in his office, that nice Burla girl! He's smart — still have a nurse and he won't have to pay her wages!"

* * *

Days came and then nights. I remained in the field with a horse and low stoneboat, loading up what stones I could find and taking them to the big white stone-pile, where I threw them off. In the darkness my mother came to me, talking in this new holy-water voice she used.

"It's night-time. You can't see what you're doing. Come on home and stop trampling the new barley shoots. The horse hasn't been out of harness since morning and father said you should have her home. So please come on!"

I felt a headache coming on, and through its scream I could hear myself shout. "So what? Drop dead, why don't you? Who's doing all the work anyway?"

She was gone, and my head cleared. I worked some more and then I slept, and when I woke up, the fields were grey with morning. My body was numb with cold. The horse had pulled the stoneboat with me on it to the hay-stack and was feeding.

* * *

I pushed my old man and he fell like a sack of potatoes, his cap rolling across the kitchen under the stove there. The old lady got down on her hands and knees to get it for him, while he lay on the floor looking at me, his toothless gums chewing on his anger. Then I started laughing and calling him names.

"You drunken old bastard! You fell by yourself — I didn't push you that hard!"

That was after Johnson, the bank manager, came over to talk to him. They went into a huddle in the corner. My old lady was going out for water, but I took the bucket from her and got it myself. When I came back into the house, my father and the banker were at it loud and wild.

"I can't pay last month's note! What in hell can I pay you with?" he was shouting at the banker.

"Then you should have thought of that before you borrowed! The bank can't afford to keep all types of bums floating! I understand there's been money for whisky, or am I wrong?"

He didn't wait for a reply, but pushed by me out the door and drove away. I asked my old man what sort of money we owed and how far behind we were in repaying. I swear that I was talking nice to him at the time — nice and low, and I was worried enough to want to get the mess straightened out somehow.

But he just looked at me like I wasn't there.

"Is it Jim?" I asked, my headache blinding me again. "Has goddamned Jim sunk us so low we've got to pay forever for it and never have a life of our own? Tell me?"

"You just keep your mouth shut where Jim's concerned! He was a good son. You're not fit to speak his name!"

He just got that out of his mouth when I gave him a shove and over he went. I might've hit him, but I can't remember. A bit of blood was coming from his mouth, and he kept looking at me.

"You fell by yourself! I didn't push you that hard!" I hollered again. She handed him his cap. I saw her hands as she was doing it, and they were shaking to beat hell. I started to cry, and when I finished they'd left the house and I felt tired enough to die.

* * *

There was nothing the matter with him that I could see, but he stayed in bed and wouldn't get up. My mother took meals in to him, but he wouldn't eat.

One night she went in to him without his supper. I'd eaten some, and was sitting at this table, knowing it was all my fault. Then I heard them arguing with her sounding off pretty strong and him only mumbling. I couldn't hear what was said because the door was shut, but I think she was throwing some of this new religious stuff at him by way of arguing something else. When she came out, I asked her to sit with me.

"I may as well go into town tomorrow and have the doctor come out to see him," I suggested. "I'll do it first thing in the morning."

"A doctor?" She looked at me as if I were crazy.

"Yes — a doctor. He hasn't eaten in three days. I was going to help get him to lunch, but he wouldn't even look at me yesterday."

She started to laugh when I said that.

"What's so funny?"

She caught her breath and choked on it.

"You're funny! A doctor for your father — there's nothing wrong with him that a doctor can cure. And because he's not sick, I won't let money be wasted on doctors for him! There shall be no more waste!"

"He's sick!"

"His sickness is in not facing up to being wrong. He's failed, and now he's scared he won't live long enough to make up for it."

"I didn't mean to push him!" I said, almost begging her to forgive. Her tired face and hunched walk that was left after the stroke seemed gone now as she stood in trembling anger. Even her breath smelled hot and furious.

"Don't you know what I'm saying?" she asked, and suddenly her voice was soft, motherly. She reached out as if to touch my face, but instead pulled back and got at the stove, throwing things here and there before she opened the fire door to put in more wood. Her back became bent again and the angry fever left her cheeks. When I next saw her face, it was again filled with her new-found religion that gave her the harmless look of the blind.

To get away from it all I figured to bury myself so deep in work that I wouldn't have the time or strength to think of anything else. When I'd finished picking stones for the season, I began putting new fences around the pasture, and getting the machinery repaired and mower sharpened for the first hay cutting. My mother didn't come out to help any more, so I was left completely alone. I only wished I could die before either of them did, to get out of it all first. I even put off going into town for grub to avoid seeing Nancy by some accident. Not that we needed that much grub — the old man did no more than nibble something every second or third day.

I tried to get through to him after she refused a doctor for him. The light was bad in his room, but it was scarey how thin and haunted he'd become even in the first few days.

"Look," I said. "I want to talk to you."

He turned away from me, and kept staring with wide-opened eyes at the wall on the other side of his bed.

"You listening?"

He didn't make like he heard me at all. I could smell the sour odour of the clothes he'd never taken off since he laid himself down.

"You planning to go like old Joe went when his church got lost on him?" I asked, trying to get him to argue at least. "I thought you said once that nothing busts a farmer down. I didn't mean to shove you — you know that!"

Still he kept staring away, and then I got sore.

"I guess if I was Jim talking, you'd listen, wouldn't you?"

I didn't want to hit him with that, but it did make him turn. The look he gave me was both angry and lost as hell itself. I felt just as sick of it all.

"Can I take you to hospital?" I was begging now. That was the last time I spoke to him.

I used to sit at this table after supper, and watch the old lady bring in her Bible. In the past, the old Bible hadn't been opened once in all the years I've lived. But now she was in it every night, following page by page, word by word with her finger, while the grease on the dishes hardened and the floor got swept only on Saturday mornings.

"What's it say that's so interesting?" I asked her one evening. She looked up at me and gave a smile I'd never seen on her face before. It was the smile of a tired woman who's going to bed at last and knows she'll not have to get up until she's had a good sleep. It was also a smile that sort of looked down at me, if you know what I mean, and I found it cutting more skin. But I didn't say anything, not even when she said:

"Each one of us must live to find the Word of God on our own, son!"

So I worked from dawn to dusk, seven days a week, trying by sheer labour to clean away the filth and guilt

135

that weighed me down like a ten-foot logging chain. And as I worked, I thought of the life I had lived and all those that had peopled it, much as I've been telling you. It made time pass, and there were moments I could smile a bit.

Nancy Burla kept troubling me in my thoughts. The more tired I became, the more she appeared to me as a Nancy Burla I did not know. She had become a temptress with no face I could recognize as belonging to her, only a body with a strong animal scent. And her body swelled until it split her clothes wide open and I had to waken and grasp my manhood in both hands and hurt it to keep from shaming myself further.

I would get out of bed gasping for air, dress myself and walk like a demon through the night, sucking in the sweat off my face through my wide-open nostrils. But even when I hurt so much that my leg and arm muscles jumped at the slightest sound, I could not help but think of her, and all I had lost with her gone from me.

Then my father died.

I guess I'd known all along he was dying, for when it happened it didn't seem to bother me at all. I felt I was in a strange town, like the cowboy song says, trying to find the gates to the country — all confused. He had passed on in his sleep, and my old lady told me before breakfast. I sat at the table and said nothing. She brought the food, and I ate like any other morning. I even had another cup of coffee. Then I went into the room to see him.

When I came out, she'd gone to tell the neighbours, or at least those that were in her new faith, as I later suspected.

I left the house then and climbed into the barn hay loft. There was a wide black poplar plank curing under the hay for I don't know how many years. It was straight as anything, hard and shiny. We'd kept it to make a new water-trough for the cattle for the time when the old one began to leak from rot.

I moved the hay over and pulled the plank down. Then I measured it carefully back and forth and sideways. The way it figured out, by cutting it short so that his head and feet touched the ends, there was enough plank there to make a casket for my father.

I began to saw away, and by night time had a crude wooden box built for him.

My mother didn't come back, so all this time I was alone with my hammering, and the blood pounding heavy in my ears. I had no hunger or thirst — no sensation of the body. Only loneliness and a desire to reach the end of whatever was to come. Once my mind began to waver and I felt I was carrying the casket on my shoulders, tripping and falling on the way to the cemetery, and the neighbours running beside me and shouting insults in my ears . . .

Hammer still in hand, I went outside. The fields seemed to fall away, turned to ashes, and the trees parched and wilted as with some great heat. Yet the air was cold and made my hot skin ache.

Night came like a silent mist, without sound or substance. I lit the lantern in the shed and worked on. By morning, my nails were broken and my fingers bled, but the casket was polished and glowing like some holy thing in the dim shed.

Still my mother did not come back.

Now I went outside, and had to shield my eyes against the red heat of the sun. I turned to the house, and saw it listing and scaley, as if it too had perished with him and had begun to rot over the decomposing body of my old man. Around me, the countryside was a desert. Not a soul came over to help or talk to me. I felt frightened as I stared at the homes dotting the ends of fields, the same houses you can see through this window and that one.

They seemed like something grown out of the dirt, as if no human had lived or loved in any of them. Sheep, cattle and dogs wandered stupidly over fields and pastures, but they seemed wild now, as if they always moved that way without master or purpose. I felt tears of panic, but choked them back. I wanted to shout out loud, "Enough!" But I had no voice anymore.

Still, like Johnson the banker, nobody tore themselves from the world beyond mine to come to me. I knew now this was the way it had to be. This was my end, and his end, and probably the same end Jim saw in that last half second before his body was broken against an English tree.

I got a shovel from the barn and started walking down the road to the burying grounds. Again I felt I had walked here before, carrying a terrible load that shifted and rolled on my shoulders. I stopped and laid down the shovel in the dust and pinched myself. I also bit my tongue.

There was pain — sharp and sweet! I was alive!

I dug wide and deep into the solid clay — through the day and into a night and then another day. A kid came off the road, leaned over to look down at me, then ran away, Now there were no thoughts of Nancy Burla.

"I have killed the animal in me! I whispered to myself over and over, knowing it was so and feeling good for it. "Now I can bury my father without shame!"

Then there were no thoughts at all, only a strange dizziness and the taste of salt in my mouth. I saw my arms, big and flashing with sweat in the sun, but not seeming to belong to me anymore.

Then it came to me — the truth I had never realized before — the truth Nancy Burla saw when she married the doctor. These arms were all I had and all that anybody had ever wanted. Anybody — my mother, those who hired stone-pickers, and Nancy Burla. They were the reason for my life. Here was my strength and my food and my bed. There was no other part of me worth anything — never had been. In so short a time they raised their Jims, their babies, their invalid mothers and fathers — and then they shrivelled and brought unhappiness to the man willing to

138

work but not able because his visions twisted downwards into a patch of earth no larger than a grave.

What price a stone-picker's ballad? What curse is his dream? What I saw and felt all these years was real — only to you, out there, was it wasted shadows on a landscape that had never been painted.

The burial casket came towards me, carried by all the neighbours who filled the road for a quarter mile as they came in twos and threes, through the cemetery gate and to the fresh grave I had dug.

Everybody was there — Wally Pantaluk, limping and leaning heavily on his stick; John, the wife-beater, carrying a trunk-sized Bible under his arm and followed by my mother who had a sacred look on her face now that she had made peace with her conscience; Shorty Mack, still dressed in a white shirt with cufflinks, and wearing a blue jacket for mourning; Mary and Pete Ruptash, who stood well back against the fence, weeping with a greater sorrow than I knew; Clem, the blacksmith, long-haired and with the tortured face of a poet-saint. They even brought dumb Andrew, who shivered as with cold and pulled his collar high around his throat. Stanley, the horse-trader came, but stayed outside the cemetery grounds. He stopped his new team of horses on the road, currying them woodenly and staring through his blind eyes in our direction. The auctioneer, who brought a fistful of paper flowers, which he dropped carelessly on the nailed-down box.

Marta Walker was there, alone with growing belly, where the child of Hector grew. Hector had gone since winter up north to Smith, where he married a farm-girl about Easter time. So Marta came alone, and I saw her staring at me with the eyes of someone who's come to a wedding rather than a funeral. For the longest time I could not break away from her eyes, in which I again saw the promise of a darkened shed and a dead dog in the yard. Big Dan Makar and Sophie, both grown handsome as statues; Minerva Malan, dark and overfed; the Bayracks came up and stood behind a few faces grown blurry to me. Then I looked to the gate, and saw Nancy Burla and Doctor Helsen coming up. By now I felt cold towards them, like a stranger grown grey.

Sergei Pushkin came and embraced my mother. He and his wife held her hands all through the burial. Pete Wilson, the store-keeper, came farthest, all the way from Calgary. Then a few people from town. There were farmers I had worked for from as far away as ten miles — some others only my folks must've known. But Pete Wilson came from farthest away . . .

I was still dressed in the milk-stained jeans and torn shirt I had worked in for over a week. I smelled of cream and straw, dust, grain and stones. But it didn't matter. It was for others to stand beside my mother now and do all the nice things that must be done. None saw me or spoke to me, except Marta, burning her sinful stare into my skull.

John droned on and on about what a good man my father had been. How he'd raised a good, God-fearing family, and how the Lord would fix up a goose-feather bed for him in paradise. Then he closed the book, and I moved forward, pushing through the small crowd over the grave, carrying my shovel in my hands. It had to end here — in this way. I heard a commotion start around and behind me, but I struggled on, my eyes on the shiny dark casket now lowered to the bottom of the hole I had dug for it.

"Stop him! He's going to throw the first sods on his father!" some woman called out. Then a man stepped in front of me.

"Hey, boy! Enough's enough — you're not to do this. Go stand by your mother an' let me do this! It's not for you to do this!"

"What's wrong?" I argued as through a dream. "I've got nothing else to do. I can do this as quick as anybody."

My voice sounded old and rusted to me.

"At a time like this you don't help. No son buries his

father when there's others to help. We didn't know before today. Go over to your mother an' take it easy!"

He tried to be a friendly and good neighbour. Before I knew what he was doing, he took my shovel from my hands, leaving me naked and useless. I grabbed for it and twisted it away from him. His eyes opened wide with surprise and then he stepped back. I heard a loud gasp from behind me as I walked over to the open grave. I began filling in the pit. If there were others helping, I do not remember, for time and memory stopped for me then.

When I looked up again, the sun was high and hot, and I ached so I straightened with terrible difficulty. Now memory came back, and feeling and hearing. I heard my old lady crying like she'd never stop. The Pushkins had left her and were standing alone. How small she looked and how pathetic! I began moving to her, to take her arm and tell her it had all ended. That we would begin as equals and try to rebuild from what was left us.

But her broken health was being fed by new spirits strange and distant to me. John, the evangelist, tried to hold me back, but I brushed him to one side. Then she saw me, and from her crying came this sharp, high scream. She turned and left the cemetery at a run, even though the doctor had said she was never to run again.

Yes, running, with her head thrown back, out the gate and up the road towards our home. The crowd moved nearer the gate, but nobody went through. As I came up, they parted to let me through first. John came up behind me, wrestling the big Bible in his arms.

"She's going to work in our hostel — it's all decided!" he said to me. I turned to him, the shovel in my hand, and he stepped away. I walked on.

"So there was no one to tell us the day he died!" an angry voice said out of the crowd. "Damn you, anyway!"

Then a woman in a soft, gentle voice: "You've done a

dark and terrible thing today!"

"Shush now, that's not so!" a man scolded her.

"Don't hold no grudge now, no matter what they've done to you. Take care of your mother and do what's right." Now it was the voice of Dan Makar, standing near the gate. I wanted to cry out that I hadn't reached the end of living. It was only the frightening beginning of another afternoon.

"You've got neighbours, boy. Where there's neighbours there's love and belonging!"

And then a voice that might've been Marta Walker. Or was it Helen Bayrack?

"It's love that'll make it all wonderful. Find love quickly — today!"

"Good luck, kid!"

I was out the gate . . . the road . . . I hurried home. Behind me the voices had had their silences for the day and now rose in louder, everyday talk. I hurried on, and the trees, fields and piles of stone along the roadside danced through the tears pouring out of my head.

That was how the day ended.

TALONBOOKS — FICTION IN PRINT 1976

Songs My Mother Taught Me — Audrey Thomas
Stories — Scott Watson
Blown Figures — Audrey Thomas
Hungry Hills — George Ryga
Theme for Diverse Instruments — Jane Rule
Mrs. Blood — Audrey Thomas
Night Desk — George Ryga
Ballad of a Stonepicker — George Ryga
Dürer's Angel — Marie-Claire Blais